KT-522-748

Snake Eyes

Newly recruited to the renowned Pinkerton Detective Agency, Finn Dexter is on leave visiting his father's ranch near Ellsworth, Kansas, when a letter received from a friend causes some concern. Ned Sullivan's son Matt has been shot and he has asked if the boy can stay on the ranch.

When Matt arrives by train the next day, a hired gunman tries to finish the job begun in Kansas City but fails for the second time. Finn goes after the killer and realizes that there is much more to this shooting than meets the eye. He heads for the city and uncovers a nest of vipers operating illegal rackets from the Snake Eyes casino, operated by Lew Faringo.

Finn must call on all his newly acquired detection skills if he is to outwit the gang and bring the real criminal mastermind to justice.

Snake Eyes

Dale Graham

A Black Horse Western

ROBERT HALE · LONDON

ISBN 978-0-7198-1491-4

Robert Hale Limited
Clerkenwell House
Clerkenwell Green
London EC1R 0HT

www.halebooks.com

Typeset by
Derek Doyle & Associates, Shaw Heath
Printed and bound in Great Britain by
CPI Antony Rowe, Chippenham and Eastbourne

ONE

HIDDEN AGENDA

Blake Dexter's craggy face screwed up into a pensive frown as he carefully reread the letter in his hand. It was from a friend in Kansas City who was campaigning for state senator in the forthcoming elections. Ned Sullivan had written asking Blake to make enquiries about an opponent of his who was visiting Ellsworth. No other information was included. So why did he want to know all about Silas Harper?

The rancher was a tall, lean-limbed man on the wrong side of fifty, whose chiselled features had many of the more mature ladies in the nearby town trembling at the knees when he walked down the street.

His wife had died two years before, snatched from him by a virulent attack of cholera. But Blake had shown no interest in pursuing any of the less than subtle propositions that came his way. Instead he had thrown all his energies into making the Circle D the most efficient cattle spread in the county.

He stood up and walked across to the large front window of the ranch house. Unconsciously his hand brushed a stray lock of iron-grey hair off his forehead. Outside, the hands were going about their daily tasks. Blake lit up a cigar and puffed on the large Havana, allowing the smoke to dribble from between pursed lips. All seemed well with the world.

But he was still troubled. Grey eyes strayed to the letter on his desk. Another frown creased his furrowed brow. Silas Harper was the current senator and he was up for re-election. Could the slippery jasper be planning some underhanded chicanery?

He wouldn't put anything past the conniving politician. Rumours of his shady practices abounded but nothing had ever been proved. Harper was a sly operator who knew how to play the political system.

Blake scowled. The intimation in the message appeared to suggest that Ned had serious reservations about Senator Harper's integrity.

'You still worried about that letter, Pa?'

The deeply rich tones were those of a younger man who had just entered the room.

'I ain't seen Ned in over a year,' replied Finn Dexter's father. 'And now, out of the blue he's asking me to investigate the credentials of Silas Harper. He says that the guy is supposedly visiting Ellsworth tomorrow on a special visit because the town is a marginal. The vote could go either way. But I ain't so sure.'

'Maybe that's all it is, an innocent visit,' Finn said. 'I reckon that suspicious nature of your'n is playing tricks again.'

Blake smiled. His face crinkled up at his son's blithe comment.

'Could be you're right, boy. Perhaps I am becoming too cynical in my old age. Although, in the past my instincts have always proved correct. I don't trust Harper.' He went on to outline some of the things in which the senator was thought to be involved. 'But it's all hearsay, mind. Nothing has ever been proved.'

Finn's handsome face darkened. Perhaps there was more to this than met the eye. He took one of the cigars from the humidor and lit up, joining Blake by the window. Father and son were very much of the same mould. Both were upright and solidly built, well able to take care of themselves, and anyone else who tried muscling in on their domain. Finn had proved his worth the previous fall when rustlers had stolen fifty head of prime beef from the east range.

Taking five of the ranch hands he had hunted them down. The gang were caught red-handed using running irons to alter the brands in a box canyon. A cabin and corrals indicated this was an enterprise that had been going on for some time. Three of the rustlers had been shot and killed when they refused to surrender. The other two quickly threw down their guns and were now serving time in the state penitentiary at Leavenworth.

Since then Finn had applied and been accepted as a trainee agent for the burgeoning Pinkerton Detective Agency. He was home on leave for a couple of weeks, his first break since joining the force. Blake had hoped that his son would partner him on the ranch. But cattle-ranching was not for the younger man. Finn's altercation with the rustlers had stimulated his desire for excitement.

Allan Pinkerton had offered him that in bucket loads.

The agency had won fame for its daring new methods in the apprehension of criminals. Its founder was dubbed *The Eye* on account of the logo and slogan: *We Never Sleep.* Only the most resourceful men were hired to undertaken the clandestine work. Their success reflected on Pinkerton, whose fame had spread nationwide.

At the interview Finn Dexter showed that he possessed the acumen and sharpness needed in a Pinkerton man. The founder of the company informed him that he did 'not know the meaning of the word "fail". Nothing in hell or heaven can influence me when I know that I am right.'

Pinkerton expected his agents to have the same dogged determination in pursuing a job to its conclusion.

But a new man was not precipitated into the field unprepared. Finn was sent on a course to study the new science of criminal detection. Once the course was completed, he partnered an experienced agent until such time as that operative considered him to be capable of independent tasks.

This vacation, he hoped, was a prelude to that assumption.

Being taken on as a detective by the celebrated agency boss was a feather in the cap of any enterprising young man. Finn Dexter was more than happy to be counted among its elite personnel. He couldn't wait to get started on his first case.

Maybe this would be it.

'Mind if'n I accompany you to Ellsworth?' Finn asked puffing on the cigar. A bloodhound rubbed its large head against his leg. Idly he stroked the dog's heavy body. 'This request from Ned sounds intriguing.'

The reservations expressed by Blake Dexter about Harper's visit had quickly been transferred to his son. A young man eager for adventure, Finn's thoughts were conjuring up all manner of dark and sinister high jinks.

Blake sensed the motivation pushing his son's line of thought. He laughed. The boy was like a chip off the old block.

'Glad to have you along,' he said, slapping the boy on the shoulder. 'We can have some lunch at Marny's Diner and make a day of it. There'll be a great atmosphere with a visiting politician in town.' An admonishing finger wagged under his son's nose. 'But don't you go trying to make out that some gigantic conspiracy is afoot, boy. It's probably as you say, just an innocent visit to drum up support for his election campaign.'

But Finn was not listening. The seed had been sown. His head was now filled with bold visions of derring-do.

'Old Ned always was a sceptical jasper,' his father continued, watching one of his hands wrestling with a wayward bronc across the yard in the corral. The guy was tossed in the air and hit the dirt with a heavy bump.

His buddies chortled uproariously. Blake Dexter joined in the good-natured hilarity. He had offered a bonus to the man who succeeded in taming that particular wild stallion. 'He thought every guy that challenged him was up to no good.'

Blake waited for a reply. Nothing was forthcoming.

'You been listening to what I've said, boy?' he admonished his preoccupied son.

'Sure did, Pa,' muttered Finn, jerking out of his reverie. 'You were laughing at Duke getting thrown off'n that feisty grey.'

Blake shook his head.

He knew exactly where his son's thoughts had been. But he said nothing. The lad had made his choice, and Blake Dexter would back him all the way. That didn't mean to say he was happy about the situation. Pinkertons were no less likely to chew on hot lead than any other lawman on the frontier.

Father and son set off alone the following morning before sunup.

The false dawn slid effortlessly above the eastern horizon in a gradually blossoming yellow glow. Soon after, the new day's sun sprang into view, the golden orb bright and scintillating. Encased in brilliant striations of purple, orange and pink, it offered a mesmerizing tableau of which the aging rancher never tired. The majestically domed silhouette of Mushroom Rock was instantly recognizable on the far side of Ellsworth. It offered a distinctive landmark to aim for.

Not that either man needed any help to locate the cattle town. They could have found their way there blindfolded.

The sound of galloping hoofs drew them to a halt close to where a probing finger of rock known as Coronado's Finger poked at the drifting skeins of cloud overhead. Blake swung round in the saddle and studied their back trail.

'Looks mighty like Windy Jim Brindle,' observed the rancher.

'And he's sure giving that mustang some lick,' Finn added. 'Wonder what can have brought him after us?'

There would be no answer to that question until the foreman reached them. Five minutes later Brindle hauled rein in a cloud of dust. The foreman of the Circle D had been with its owner since the beginning. They had been through the war together and come up the trails from Texas before Blake decided it would much easier and more profitable to establish a spread close to the railroad.

'Why are you in such an all-fired rush, Windy?' asked Blake. 'Some'n wrong back at the ranch?' Brindle dug into his pocket and brought out a letter.

'This arrived by pony express soon after you left the ranch this morning, boss,' the foreman gabbled, handing it across. 'Ella figured it might be important so she sent me after you.'

Ella Dexter was Blake's sister who had come West to support her elder brother, following the bereavement. She had stayed on to look after the books and do any paperwork.

11

The rancher frowned down at the envelope, noting that it had been posted from Kansas City. He quickly extracted the single sheet of paper and read the missive.

'Good thing you caught us up, Windy.' Blake praised his trusted foreman. 'Seems like Ned Sullivan is sending his son on the next train.' He paused, a dark cloud of concern pinching at the leathery contour of his face. 'He wants me to put him up for a few weeks. The kid has gotten himself in some kind of trouble and been shot. Ned wants him out of the way during the election campaign.'

'Does he say what sort of trouble?' asked Finn, trying to stifle his eagerness for more information.

Blake shook his head, handing the letter across for his son to read. It sure was a mystery. Finn's eyes glittered. Things were looking up. Perhaps, after all, he was going to be pitched into the exciting life for which he craved earlier than expected.

'Much obliged for bringing this out here.' Blake thanked his foreman. 'Let Ella know that we'll be having a guest to stay. But don't tell her the reason. No sense in causing any worry until we know all the facts.'

'Sure thing, boss. You can count on me.' Windy swung his quarter horse around and pounded off back the way he had come.

As the two men continued on their way all manner of lurid ideas were sifting through Finn's animated brain. His father was more taciturn. No sense attempting to fathom out the reasoning behind young Matt's implied disgrace before they learned the facts from the kid himself.

And that would have to wait until the following day.

TWO

BACKSHOOTER

They arrived in Ellsworth to find the town in a fever of excitement. The imminent arrival of Silas Harper was a first. No other politician of his standing had ever visited the town previously. This was his last call before returning to Kansas City.

The council intended to make a show of the prospective senator's vote-catching trip in order to place the town firmly on the Kansas map. Impress one candidate and others would follow. That would mean extra business for Ellsworth. The council knew that the cattle business was shifting further west along with the expanding rail link towards the new boom town of Dodge City.

Many of the town's permanent residents would be pleased to see an end to the rowdy behaviour of the cowboys. Others, particularly the saloon owners, were more concerned about the loss of trade.

14

Bunting was being erected along the main street to welcome the visitor. A band was marching up and down practising *The Star Spangled Banner* and other patriotic tunes. All the talk was about Harper's visit. A party atmosphere was in the air with everybody looking forward to a good old shindig.

Much to the delight of local kids the school was to be closed for the day, so that they could attend the celebrations. A street party with all manner of food and drink paid for by the council was expected to attract a host of incomers from the surrounding homesteads.

Blake and his son jogged down the middle of the street.

'Sure is gonna be one humdinger of a carnival,' announced Finn, who was looking forward to joining in the festivities.

'These people might not be so eager to welcome Harper if'n they knew the truth about him,' snorted his father. 'The guy's a slippery chiseller who has the means to cover his tracks.'

'You figure that young Matt might have got involved in something crooked and that was the reason he was shot?' Finn asked eager for more details.

Blake shrugged. 'We'll find out soon enough when he arrives on the train tomorrow.' Then he changed the subject. 'Let's get booked into the Prairie Oyster Hotel before all the rooms are taken.'

Finn hadn't considered that. Neither of them had any wish to spend the night sleeping on a hard bench in the station waiting room. The Oyster was the best hotel in town. More expensive, but worth every penny.

Each of the de luxe rooms had a bath tub and fully sprung beds. There was even an indoor latrine and complimentary barber's shop for use of the guests. Most important as far as Blake Dexter was concerned, it boasted Ellsworth's finest restaurant supervised by a gourmet chef brought all the way from France.

Their luck was out, however. All the rooms had been commandeered for the Harper delegation.

'Ain't that typical,' grumbled Blake. 'Harper gets all the best attention while the voters are left with the leavings.' Finn couldn't help but chuckle at his father's sense of aggrievement.

They soon found a suitable room at the less flamboyant but comfortable National Hotel. As soon as they were settled in and a table had been reserved at Marny's, both men headed across the street to the marshal's office.

Hangdog Charlie Mancos was slouched in a chair, struggling over some paperwork that needed completing before the next day. The grouchy look that had resulted in his nickname brought a grin to Blake's face.

'You look kinda down in the dumps, Charlie,' the rancher commented, struggling to contain the smirk.

The lawman huffed as a bemused eye focused accusingly upon the list of figures he was studying. Then, uttering a snorting curse, he snapped the ledger shut.

'Darned paperwork,' he railed. 'The curse of my life. I became a lawman to catch villains, not sit behind a desk pen-pushing.' His next remark was for Blake. 'Any chance that fine sister of your'n could help me out?'

'Sorry, Charlie. Looking after my affairs is a full-time job.'

The marshal grunted. 'I'll have to persuade the council to hire an accountant then. Next time I see the mayor I'm gonna mention it.'

Blake received the same diatribe every time he called on his old friend. Each time he gave the same answer.

'You do that, Hangdog. Let 'em see who's boss.'

The marshal nodded in agreement. 'Durned right I will.' Then he opened a drawer and removed a bottle of whisky. Three glasses were poured, the men toasting each other's health.

'So what can I do for you boys today?' Mancos said, smacking his lips in appreciation of the fine Scotch.

'Have you heard if'n Silas Harper is here for any special reason?' Blake asked, offering the marshal a fat cigar. Mancos considered the query before replying.

'Far as I know it's just a goodwill visit to encourage folks to place their cross against his name in the elections. This is a marginal seat. All the big shots have been here this month.' Hangdog paused to light up the cigar. Blue smoke spiralled in the still air. 'Have you some other information I should know about?'

Blake shook his head. 'Just wondering, is all. Thought maybe the devious varmint had some secret plan up his sleeve.'

'Take it from me, Blake. It's just a simple vote-catching tour. He's staying here a couple of days, then heading back to Kansas City. Anything else being planned for Ellsworth and I'd have heard about it.'

The marshal turned to address his next remark to

17

Finn. 'Can't you keep this old cuss from thinking every politician has a rat stuck down his britches?'

Laughs all round greeted this declaration as the talk shifted to other more prosaic topics. The price of beef along with the growing importance of Dodge City was a prime topic of conversation. Mancos was particularly interested to learn about Finn's post with the Pinkerton Agency.

Once that had been exhausted, Hangdog told them about a new show opening the following week at the Blue Bell Theatre. It had received excellent reviews in the *Kansas Tribune*, especially with regard to the lead dancer, a French gal called Mimi La Belle.

'Although she'll have to be some'n special to best the one who's just finished. That Candy Stockwell sure is a tasty peach. If'n I was only twenty years younger. . . .' The old lawman's eyes misted over.

After much cajoling Blake agreed to accompany his buddy to the opening night.

'Bring Ella along if'n you like.' The marshal's casual postscript brought a wry smirk to the mouths of both father and son. Ella Dexter was a handsome woman whom any man would be proud to have on his arm.

Next morning the town was buzzing. Folks were up and about even before the first rooster had opened up the proceedings. The Dexters were awakened by the constant movement along the street outside the hotel. A welcome lie-in following their overindulgence at the King Pin saloon was impossible.

And there was still three hours to go before the train

from Kansas City was due in.

Time passed quickly in a ferment of activity as last-minute checks were made to welcome the important visitor. Harper's supporters were already firmly established in place to ensure they held the most prominent position when the train pulled into the station. The band was lined up on the opposite side of the track ready to strike up when given the order.

On the station platform itself a raised stage had been erected, with banners and flags in evidence where the town council, led by the mayor, was to welcome their guest.

At ten o'clock precisely the haunting sound of the locomotive whistle heralded the arrival of the east-bound train. As it pulled into the station all eyes were fixed on the portly figure standing on the viewing platform of a specially bedecked coach in the middle of the train.

Silas Harper raised a languid hand to the crowd, which erupted in a frenzy of cheering. Led by an animated conductor, the Ellsworth Brass Band commenced to play. Flags in support of the visiting official waved back and forth. Joining the chaotic mêlée were numerous hats, thrown into the air by those caught up in the frenetic excitement of the occasion.

The regular passengers descended in something of a daze, quickly hurrying away to attend their own affairs. Those remaining on the train were drawn to the side where Senator Harper was revelling in the attention.

'Keep your eyes peeled for a tall young *hombre* with his arm in a sling,' Blake advised his son. In all the cacophony they could easily miss the boy. Avidly they searched the crowd as the various dignitaries, led by the mayor, stepped forward to welcome Senator Harper and his party.

Another person was also searching for the slight figure of Matt Sullivan. While the guard was busy ushering the visitors off the train, Cash Nagle had taken advantage of his absence to enter the caboose at the rear end of the train.

This was the private domain of the guard and was usually kept locked. Caught up in the excitement of the occasion, he had omitted to secure it. This omission provided Cash Nagle with a simple access that he would otherwise have found more taxing. A small, mousy individual, Nagle wore a mustard-coloured check suit. A grey derby was planted on his head. Such apparel gave him the respectable appearance needed by a man in his profession.

Cash Nagle was a hired assassin posing as a travelling salesman.

A half-smile twisted his wily features.

'This is going to be easier than expected,' the gunman muttered to himself. From his elevated position he had quickly spotted the tall figure of Matt Sullivan walking away from the train. The killer raised his Winchester and poked it out of the back window.

As the train shuddered into motion, he took careful aim. His finger slowly and deliberately squeezed the trigger.

'Over there, Pa.' Finn pointed to a lean wiry youth walking away from the station. 'That must be him.'

Blake followed the pointing finger. 'Yep! That's young Matt all right.'

The two men stepped across to greet their guest. Blake held out his hand.

'Good to see you, Matt. I got the letter from your pa— What the—?'

The rifle shot was drowned out by the raucous hallooing of the lively crowd. The first Blake knew that something was wrong was when Matt threw his arms into the air and fell to the ground.

'What in blue blazes is going on?' exclaimed Finn, drawing his pistol. A blossoming spread of blood on the back of Matt Sullivan's shirt was his answer. The sudden attack had taken them both completely by surprise. Finn spun on his boot heels. Hunkered down into the classic gunfighter's stance, he tried to locate the source of the bushwhacking. But there was no clue to help him.

Meanwhile the train was pulling further away from the station platform. In all the furore, the shot from Cash Nagle's gun had gone completely unnoticed by anybody.

Numbed from the shock, Blake Dexter bent over the still form. The boy was not dead, but he was badly injured.

'Take it easy, son,' murmured Blake. He looked around in desperation as stunned bystanders looked on, mesmerized by the sudden violence in their midst.

'Someone get the doc!' Blake's panic-stricken shout was aimed at nobody in particular.

The boy groaned. He tried to speak. 'Ha ...

Harper. . . .' Then he lapsed into unconsciousness.

'What do you make of that?' Blake asked his son.

'Could be the bullet was meant for Harper. . . ?'

'Or Harper had something to do with it.' Blake interjected acidly.

'Either way, we'll not learn the truth of the matter until Matt comes round.'

Luckily, Doc Turner was amongst the crowd and quickly hurried across to tend the injured man. After examining the wound his craggy face assumed a grave aspect.

'It's serious, Blake. I need to get him to my place pronto so's I can remove this hunk of lead in his back. Another inch and it would have ruptured his heart. As things stand, it's gonna be touch and go whether he survives.'

Three men were quickly commandeered to carry the injured visitor to the doctor's surgery. Meanwhile Finn had picked up on the medic's observation that Matt had been shot in the back.

His gaze moved towards the rapidly disappearing train. Finn's detecting skills cranked into play.

'Looks like the shot has come from the train. The killer must have waited until the last moment before he opened fire.'

'That must mean he's still on the train,' snapped Blake. A mean and hungry look flushed his leathery features. 'I want that gunman caught,' he ordered. 'You go after him, Finn. Bring the skunk back here.'

Finn hurried off to seek out the station master and determine where the train made its next stop. It was mighty suspicious that Harper just happened to be on the same train as Matt and the assassin. Coincidence or what? That would have to be figured out later. Meanwhile he needed to get after that train.

'It has to make a temporary halt at Rock Springs to take on water,' the station master informed him. 'That is thirty miles up the line. The train will wait there on the branch line for about a half-hour to let the east-bound express through.'

Finn considered the task before him. On the flat plains to the west of Ellsworth the train could get up a full head of steam. There was no way that he could catch up with it in time, even with a half-hour stopover. His face creased in frustration.

'You could take the short cut over Salt Creek Bluffs,' Blake informed his son. 'The train has to take a longer route, sticking with the level ground. But you would reach Rock Springs in time by cutting through Soloman Gap.'

Finn had never been that way before, so he had to wait impatiently for his father to explain the directions before he could leave. Satisfied that he knew the way, Finn stressed that the killer would not escape.

Then he dug in his boot heels, urging the roan mare to a gallop. Already the train was out of sight. But the smoke billowing from the tall stack told Finn how far ahead the train had reached.

As Finn Dexter left Ellsworth Marshal Mancos hurried across from the Prairie Oyster, where he had been assisting the council with Senator Harper's stay-over. The ageing lawman was wheezing on account of

23

the unaccustomed display of exercise.

'I only just heard about the shooting,' he gasped out, sucking air into his lungs. 'Any idea who did it?'

'Some gunman on the train drilled poor old Matt Sullivan in the back,' rapped Blake. 'Finn's gone after him.'

'I'd have done the job myself,' the lawman gingerly apologized. The hangdog expression was clearly in evidence. 'But I'm only a town marshal. Anything beyond the limits is outside my jurisdiction.' He shrugged his shoulders ruefully before perking up with another suggestion. 'What I can do is wire the law office in the next town to search the train when it stops.'

Blake responded with an irritated shake of the head.

'That ain't no darned use. The varmint will have left the train well before then.'

'Could be you're right, Blake. But I'll do it anyway,' Mancos said, trying to smooth over the delicate situation. 'Sorry I can't offer more help. It's a good job that boy of yourn has signed up with the Pinkertons. Those guys don't have such limitations on their actions.'

Mancos scowled. 'I'm getting a mite too old for this kinda stuff. Figured the wild days were over and done with so's I could see out my last years in peace. Ain't so sure now. You remember what they used to say about Ellsworth back in '72?'

'I sure do,' Blake concurred. 'Abilene the first, Dodge City the last, and Ellsworth the wickedest. Sure hope them wild times don't return.'

Hangdog nodded in forlorn agreement. 'Let's check up on young Sullivan at the doc's surgery,' he grunted.

'Then I'll be ready for a drink.'

'Reckon I'll join you in that, Charlie.' Blake didn't blame Hangdog for the shooting. He knew that the marshal's hands were tied.

The two buddies sauntered off up the street, both hoping and praying that the victim of the untimely violence was still in the land of the living.

THREE

SNAKE ON A TRAIN

Cash Nagle, meanwhile, was having to think quickly.
The guard had returned to the caboose sooner than
expected. He was hammering on the door, which he'd
realized too late had been left unlocked. Nagle had
wedged it shut with a lump of wood.

'Who's in there?' came the blunt demand from
Amos Kegan, the guard as he struggled to open the
door. 'Better let me in now or you'll be in serious
trouble.'

Nagle quickly hid the rifle behind some packing
cases.

'Hold on a minute, mister,' he called back. 'The
door seems to be stuck.' Shuffling about he then kicked
the wedge free so that it slid into a corner.

Next moment Kegan burst in. His thick grey moustache bristled with indignation as he tried to keep his

26

cool. After all, the guy was unarmed and a paying passenger. He lowered his gruff voice to a more appeasing tone.

'What goes on here, sir? This is a private area,' he declared. 'It's against company rules for passengers to enter the caboose.'

'Sorry about that,' Nagle apologized. 'I just came in here to check on my luggage. I had no idea it was off limits.'

The elderly guard accepted the excuse, then ushered him into the adjoining carriage before returning to the caboose. His bulbous nose wrinkled. The acrid tang of burnt powder still hung in the air.

'Something ain't right here,' Kegan muttered under his breath while searching the van. The distinctive odour soon led him to the packing cases at the rear, where he found Nagle's rifle. There was no proof that the guy had used it. But somebody sure had. Perhaps he'd been potting at deer from the viewing platform. So why offer the lame excuse that he was checking his luggage? It didn't make sense. Kegan's thick eyebrows met in the middle. The jasper was hiding something.

After replacing the rifle behind the cases the guard returned to the main carriages. A suspicious glower wrinkled his gnarled features. This particular passenger needed careful watching. Amos Kegan then continued with his normal duties, giving no hint that he harboured reservations about the sly Nagle.

The killer was given a false sense of security, which he soon put into practice. Unaware that he was under observation, Nagle waited until the guard had moved into the next carriage. A few minutes passed while he satisfied himself that the guard was otherwise engaged. Then he stood up and returned to the caboose.

His aim was to retrieve the used rifle and clean it at the earliest opportunity. Once that was done he would be in the clear.

Kegan gave him a moment, then followed. Hiding at the far end of the last carriage he saw the guy slipping into the caboose.

A deep breath helped to calm taut nerves before the guard hustled along the centre aisle back to the caboose. Gingerly he pushed open the door. Nagle was delving behind the packing cases.

'You have some serious explaining to do, mister,' snapped the guard. 'And if'n I ain't satisfied you'll be handed over to the sheriff when we reach Abilene.'

Taken by surprise, Nagle soon recovered his composure. He swung to face the guard, levering a fresh round into the chamber of his rifle.

'That's what you think,' Nagle growled back. He was about to haul back on the trigger before realizing that that was out of the question. A rifle shot would alert the other passengers, which was the last thing the gunman needed.

Without waiting for a reply the intruder launched himself at the ageing guard. His rifle swung in a wide arc, cracking against Kegan's head. The old guy didn't stand a chance. He dropped to the floor of the caboose.

A quick tug to open the sliding door followed. With the prairie wind blowing his wispy brown hair, Nagle glanced along the outside of the carriages to ensure that nobody was watching from one of the forward viewing platforms. Satisfaction that his skulduggery would pass unobserved elicited a mirthless smile.

He was now ready to dispose of the unconscious guard. Kegan was only slightly built and it took little effort for the blackguard to push the inert body out of the chugging train. It bounced a couple of times down the low embankment before juddering to a halt.

Nobody would discover the body until he was well away.

'That'll teach you to meddle in Cash Nagle's affairs,' the braggart muttered under his breath as he closed the door.

The train sped on towards Rock Springs, its passengers completely oblivious to the heinous deed so recently perpetrated in their midst.

The short cut that Finn Dexter had taken was so that he could reach Rock Springs before the train left the small junction. That would have given him ample time to board the westbound and search for the bushwhacker. But things do not always work out as planned. On this occasion it was an unexpected encounter that delayed him.

As he crested a low hillock the final stretch of line five miles east of Rock Springs came into view. The train had already passed but wisps of smoke curling into the sky could still be detected. Urging his horse to increase its pace, the rider had every hope of reaching the junction in time.

Then he noticed a movement beside the track.

What in blue blazes had happened here? He swung right, urging the roan down the grassy slope. Realization soon dawned that the alien hump was a human being. The guy must have somehow fallen off the train and not been spotted. Drawing closer he could see that the man was wearing a uniform.

Finn jumped off his horse and bent down beside the supine form. Thankfully the guy was still breathing. But he was in bad shape. His arm was bent at an angle indicating that it had been broken. Numerous cuts and abrasions also needed attention. Following a quick appraisal, Finn was relieved that, otherwise, the old dude's life did not appear to be under threat.

Gently he levered him up. A few gentle words of encouragement and Amos Kegan's eyes slowly flickered open. His dirt-smeared face creased in pain when he tried to move. Finn eased him back down. Seen close up, it was obvious that he was the train guard. So how had he come to be lying beside the track, his dire predicament apparently unknown to the rest of the train's complement?

Finn's brow furrowed with unease. This looked mighty strange. Mighty strange indeed. He unhooked his canteen and dribbled water into the guard's mouth.

'Much obliged, young fella,' Kegan gurgled. 'Thought I was a goner ... when that skunk attacked me in the caboose.'

Finn stiffened. So he had been right. There was much more to this than met the eye. Maybe the fella who had slugged the guard, and Matt Sullivan's back-shooter were one and the same.

SNAKE EYES

'What happened?' Finn enquired. The story was related briefly in fits and starts.

'Sounds like the pesky galoot I'm after,' Finn murmured.

Carefully, Finn helped the old guard to his feet. 'Think you can climb up on to my saddle? I'll get you to Rock Springs, but we'll have to ride double.'

Soon after, the duo were heading along the trackside. The pace was considerably slower than Finn would have preferred, due to the guard's injuries.

Halfway to Rock Springs the eastbound express clattered past, the engineer offering the riders a rousing toot on his whistle. Finn tipped his hat in acknowledgement. Sitting upfront with Finn's arms encircling him, Amos Kegan was more intent on holding on. His broken arm pained something rotten. And no matter how careful Finn was to keep his horse steady, jolts and wrenches were inevitable.

After what seemed like a coon's age to the injured guard, they arrived at Rock Springs. The railroad junction only had a station where the man in charge resided, plus a large water tower.

Finn arranged for the injured guard to rest up in the quarters occupied by the sole occupant of the tiny station. Lonesome Jake Varley was more than willing to accommodate his old buddy.

'What happened to you, Amos?' he said, fussing around his unexpected guest. It was Finn who provided all the answers.

Kegan had lost a lot of blood and needed a doctor. The nearest one was at the next town along the line.

31

The next train heading that way was not due for another five hours. Varley soon had the guard's cuts and bruises bandaged up. The broken arm was carefully set in a sling until such time as a real sawbones could take over. Finn was impressed.

Once attended to, old Amos fell into a deep sleep.

With his responsibility to the injured man taken care of, Finn was anxious to learn if anybody had left the train at Rock Springs.

'Funny you should mention that, mister,' the station master replied, scratching his balding pate. 'One guy did get off. It was unusual, cos we don't have many passengers wanting to hang around admiring the beautiful scenery hereabouts.' His arm encompassed the endless rolling prairie grassland that changed little whichever way you looked.

Finn's ears pricked up. 'Can you describe him?'

'A little mousy sort of guy, wearing a mustard suit. Acted kinda fidgety.'

'Where did he go from here?' asked Finn.

'That's another strange thing,' murmured the bemused station master. 'He bought a ticket to go right back where he'd just come from. The eastbound always stops here for water. I didn't question him about it. Takes all sorts to make a world, I guess.' He threw a searching look at the tall Pinkerton. 'You acquainted with this dude?'

'You could say. He shot a guy in Ellsworth then escaped on the train. The guard was thrown off the same train when he became too inquisitive. I reckon this fella thought that was the end of him.'

32

'He sure was edgy,' added an animated Jake Varley. 'He could hardly wait for the eastbound to pull in. You must have passed it on your way here.'

Finn nodded. Now that he had discovered the whereabouts of the gunman, he wanted to get on his way pronto. But the ride from Ellsworth over the Salt Creek Bluffs had tired his horse. Even though the delay was frustrating, a short respite was essential to re-energize both man and beast.

Varley was more than eager to have a guest with whom he could chew the fat. They retired to his office, where a fresh bottle of hooch was duly uncorked. Some home-made cookies were also produced to while away the hour's rest that Finn reckoned was needed.

The station master proved to be an enthusiastic talker. He worked a two week shift returning to his permanent home in Pine Ridge for a short break when a replacement took over. The living quarters were basic, but Varley made sure he lacked for nothing. Everything he needed came in by train, all at the company's expense.

And he enjoyed the solitary existence.

'Folks call me Lonesome. They figure a guy that spends most of his life out here must be a miserable hermit.' Varley shook his head. 'It ain't so. There are plenty of trains passing through, so a guy always has company,' he explained to Finn after checking that old Amos was comfortable.

Living out here in the boondocks, Varley had become adept at a host of tasks that most folks took for granted. Hence his skill at dealing with Kegan's injuries and producing some tasty comestibles.

He went on to explain that the other line, branching off at the junction, headed west, where it terminated at Hayes.

'The Atchison Topeka Company intend to push on towards Dodge City.' Varley went across to a cupboard and brought back some freshly baked biscuits. Finn smiled. He could readily understand why the lonesome station master had achieved his rotund figure. 'Their eventual destination is Santa Fe in New Mexico. There's a heap of trade being carried on down there, but the wagon trail is hard and dangerous. The first railroad to get there will make a mint of dough.'

Lonesome Jake could have gone on chatting all day. But Finn was eager to depart.

'Much obliged for your hospitality, Lonesome,' he said, thanking the station master after refusing yet another of his delicious biscuits. 'I'd be obliged if'n you could send a wire to me via the marshal's office in Ellsworth about the guard's condition.'

'Sure thing, Finn,' Varley assured his guest. 'And good luck in your hunt for this lowlife varmint.'

A wave and the Pinkerton man was spurring off back the way he had come.

When Finn arrived back in Ellsworth he went straight to the hotel. His father had been on tenterhooks ever since his son left the town on his perilous quest.

'Boy, am I glad to see you back safe and sound,' he declared, ushering his son into their room. 'How did things pan out?'

34

Finn went on to apprise his father of all that had happened; the finding of the injured train guard, his meeting with the Rock Springs station master and, most important, the fact that the hired gunman had returned to Ellsworth.

Blake Dexter was baffled as to why the guy had returned to the scene of his crime.

'He must have come back to collect his payout from the skunk that hired him,' snarled Finn. 'Do you figure it could be Harper?'

'I wouldn't put it past him,' Blake said. 'Trouble is, we can't prove it until we find the gunman.' He walked around the small room, a thoughtful expression clouding his rugged features. 'And how we gonna find one man amongst all the cowpokes and drifters in town, not to mention all of Harper's supporters? The town's bursting at the seams. He's been strutting around all day like a stuffed rooster shaking hands and offering free drinks to drum up more support.'

Finn stroked his square chin. 'The varmint must be staying in one of the smaller hotels so as not to arouse any suspicion until he's been paid off. And I have a good description of him from the train guard.' He clapped his father on the shoulders. 'Don't worry, Pop. If'n the rat is in Ellsworth we'll flush him out.'

His son's optimistic attitude lifted the older man's spirits.

'The sooner we get started the better. There can't be that many places for a guy to bed down in a town the size of Ellsworth.'

FOUR

NO PAY FOR CASH

Before starting out on their search for Cash Nagle, the two men went across to see how Matt Sullivan was bearing up. They found that he was still unconscious. Doc Turner didn't beat about the bush.

'It's a miracle he ain't dead, boys. But he's young and his condition has settled down. With careful handling and plenty of rest there is no reason why he shouldn't pull through.' The medic had done all he could for the young man. Now all they could do was hope, and wait for Matt to recover.

'If anyone can bring him round it'll be you, Doc. You've done your best, whatever happens. I'm just dreading having to tell his pa about all this.' Blake's woebegone expression elicited a nod of sympathy from the sawbones. Only time would tell whether the youngster would pull through and let them know the cause of his strife.

Before leaving Doc Turner's surgery Finn impressed upon the medic the necessity of telling anybody who came enquiring after his health that Matt Sullivan had passed away and had never recovered consciousness.

'That way the killer will figure he's done a proper job. It gives us an edge.'

Back on the main street of Ellsworth, Finn knew that the first thing they needed to do was determine whether the gunman had in fact got off the train. They found the ticket collector eating his supper in the station office.

'Nobody of that description got off the train here.' The official was surly and disobliging, a regular ornery cuss.

'You certain about that, mister?'

'Ain't I just said,' snapped the churlish railroad employee. 'Nobody of that description got off the eastbound. Now beat it while I finish my supper.'

'There's no need for that sort of attitude,' Blake Dexter grumbled. 'We're only making enquiries. The varmint we're after is a hired gunslinger.'

The ticket collector merely grunted.

Finn's hackles were raised, as was his suspicion that the guy was hiding something. And he couldn't abide snide remarks from public officials. Never one to beat about the bush, he grabbed the collector by his shirt and hauled him up off his seat.

'You're lying,' he rasped in the guy's ear. 'And unless you tell us the truth, I'll wipe the floor with your miserable hide. Savvy?' A meaty fist rose and paused in readiness to deliver the threatened chastisement. 'Now out with it. Did the guy we're after step down here?'

That was enough for the scrawny runt, whose evening meal was strewn over the floor. Harvey Maggs was no hero. And this burly critter looked as if he could hammer nails into a fence with his bare fists.

'OK, OK,' he stuttered out. 'Maybe there was a g-guy wearing a mustard suit got off the train. He paid me ten bucks to deny I'd seen him. That sure ain't enough to pay for any doctoring bills.'

Blake laid a restraining hand on his son's arm. He was well aware that Finn was a powerful guy more than capable of dealing out rough treatment when needed.

'Leave it, son. We found out what we came for. Now let's go find the rat.'

But Finn was not finished yet. 'Did this rat say where he was staying?' The collector shook his head. A squeeze on the frightened official's windpipe elicited a gurgle. Finn uttered a final threat.

'Mention this visit to anybody,' he hissed out, 'and the sawbones will be extra busy tonight.' Then he tossed the guy aside. Maggs's heart was beating a rapid tattoo inside his chest as he scrabbled around on the floor trying to retrieve the remnants of his supper.

The two searchers wandered outside. But before commencing their hunt for the elusive bushwhacker Finn was in need of a cold drink of beer following his hard ride back from Rock Springs. They headed for the nearest saloon across the street.

The two men were so intent on discussing their quest for Cash Nagle that they failed to notice someone who had been following them.

Spike Dobey had pegged the two men when they left their hotel. He was an expert at covert shadowing, and the two marks remained totally unaware that they were under scrutiny. Following them after they'd left the doc's surgery and visited the station master, Dobey's probing gaze watched them enter the Cactus Wren saloon.

He rightly assumed that the two men would be in there long enough for him to check on the progress of Matt Sullivan. His boss was worried that the kid would spill the beans if'n he pulled through. Dobey had firm instructions to ensure that a recovery was not on the cards.

He knocked on the door of the surgery. Moments later it was answered by Doc Turner.

'Can I help you?' the medic asked.

Slapping on his most compassionate and sensitive expression, Dobey tentatively asked in a low voice,

'I am here as a representative from the railroad company. We were very sorry to hear that one of our passengers has been shot and injured. The Kansas Pacific cares deeply about the welfare of its clients. My principals have sent me to determine how he is faring, doctor?'

Turner was completely fooled by the apparent sincerity of the bogus official. He was just about to reveal that, although badly injured, the boy was expected to recover when he remembered Finn's warning. Even though this dude looked genuine, the doctor stuck to his instruction from the Pinkerton agent.

'I regret that Mr Sullivan died in his sleep an hour ago.'

'Did he regain consciousness at all? We need to tell the next of kin.' Dobey could barely contain his elation. This was good news.

'No. The gunshot was too severe. He never uttered a word.'

Head bowed in sorrow, Dobey expressed his regrets, then left. He made certain to keep his shoulders hunched in dejection until he was no longer in view of the surgeery. The snoop then strode purposefully along the street to await the departure of Finn Dexter and his father from the Cactus Wren.

He didn't have long to wait. Ten minutes later the two men shouldered through the doors of the saloon to begin their search. They were closely followed by Dobey who knew that sooner or later they were bound to strike gold.

There weren't that many hotels and dosshouses in Ellsworth, so the task ought not to take them long. After visiting the sixth place with no luck, Blake Dexter was starting to fear that the guy they sought had already left town by horse. He voiced his concern to Finn.

'There's one more at the end of town,' his son replied. 'If'n he ain't there, we'll have to think again. But I got me a feeling about this place.' He scratched his left ear. 'When that happens, I know some'n is about to blow.'

They wandered across to the Jackdaw Hotel. It was a second-rate rooming-house catering to salesmen and other itinerant drifters. A cheap joint, it had suited

Nagle's false image perfectly until he was paid off. Then he intended spending those greenbacks on some well-earned rest in Kansas City.

At first the proprietor was reluctant to assist. Only when Finn produced his Pinkerton card and revealed that he was hunting down the man who had shot a train passenger that very morning was he persuaded to cooperate. He pointed out a guy sitting at a table who matched the description given by Finn. The fella had signed in as Cash Nagle and had been the only person to book in that day. The two men glanced across.

'Sure looks like the guy we're after,' said Finn. 'Much obliged. We'll just go over and have a quiet word with him.'

He refrained from adding that *how* quiet would depend on the critter's reaction to being challenged.

Nagle was hunched over a glass of beer. He appeared to be waiting for somebody. It was also clear that he was edgy. A nervous peeper flicked across to the clock on the wall. The delivery man was late. The hired gunslinger had a horse ready outside, and was anxious to hit the trail. The longer he stayed in this berg, the more chance there was of being rumbled.

The first thing that told Nagle he was in trouble was a tall rangy dude blocking out the dim light cast by a tallow lamp. A gruff voice asked if he had arrived on the eastbound train.

Nagle was caught unawares by the question. But, ever the consummate professional, his face remained blank, devoid of expression.

'I have come to Ellsworth by horse,' he replied evenly. Fixing the newcomers with a lofty expression he added, 'I don't see that my being here has anything to do with you.'

'You're saying that you weren't in Rock Springs today and know nothing about the unlawful killing of two men?' Finn failed to add that both victims were still alive.

'You're barking up the wrong tree, mister,' rasped Nagle, who was rapidly losing his cool. 'I don't know what you're talking about. Now clear off. I'm expecting company.'

'That stub in your hatband looks mighty like a railroad ticket,' suggested Finn. 'Maybe I should take a looksee.'

Nagel realized that his cover was blown and he needed to act. As Finn leaned across to grab the ticket, the gunman reached into his side pocket and produced a small up-and-over derringer – a lethal weapon at close quarters.

From his position to one side, Blake spotted the surreptitious move.

'Look out! He's got a gun.' The sharp warning came in the nick of time. Finn knocked the guy's arm aside just as the gun exploded. The bullet hissed past his head and shattered a window. But Nagle was not finished yet.

It was the proprietor of the Jackdaw who saved Finn's bacon. He crept up behind the gunman with a cudgel clutched in his hand. Before Nagle could raise the derringer for a second time, the heavy club connected with

42

his bullet head and laid him out.

Finn dragged the unconscious guy up and sat him back down in his seat.

'Seems I'm mighty beholden to you, mister,' he commended the hotel owner. 'That was a close thing.'

'I don't want this place becoming a refuge for gunslingers and riff-raff,' the guy intoned. 'I got my reputation to consider.'

'This ticket was like we figured,' Blake remarked. 'It's one-way from Rock Springs to Ellsworth. This is the guy, all right.'

'We still need to find out why he shot Matt,' said Finn, having secured the derringer. He addressed his next request to the proprietor. 'A jug of water, if'n you please.'

Finn handed the full jug to his father.

'I'm gonna enjoy this,' the older man breezed, taking aim.

The cold dousing was enough to bring the comatose gunslinger out of his stupor. He gurgled and coughed, cursing the sudden and objectionable restoration of his faculties.

'What the heck. . . ?'

He tried to stand up but was unceremoniously pushed back into his chair. A deadly Colt .45 pointed at his head.

'Now listen up good, mister,' growled Finn, fixing the skunk with a regard that brooked no dissent. 'You're going to tell me why you shot Matt Sullivan.'

Nagle tried denying the accusation. Finn grabbed him by the lapels of his coat and jerked him to his feet.

'That old man you threw off'n the train survived and he can identify you. Now spill the beans.'

Finn raised his meaty fist, drawing it back ready to deliver a hefty pile-driver. Nagle knew that the game was up. His eyes bulged with fear. All he could do now was spill what he knew and hope for a reduced sentence.

'OK, I'll tell you what I know,' he warbled disconsolately. 'Just give me a drink to steady my nerves.'

Finn gestured for his father to pour the guy a glass of whiskey.

Meanwhile, outside the broken window, Spike Dobey had seen and heard everything. His hand palmed the trusted Smith & Wesson Schofield. There could be only one response to this situation.

Cash Nagle looked from one to the other of his grim-faced accusers. Then he began to open up.

'I was hired in Kansas City to follow him out here on the train and finish the job off.'

'Who hired you?' This was the crucial question. They needed the answer to that in order to nail Mister Big.

Nagle opened his mouth, but all that emerged was a choking cry as he tumbled forward. He had been shot in the back through the window. All the other occupants of the hotel's common room ducked down.

Finn was the first to recover, scrambling crablike over to where Nagle had fallen. But the guy was dead. The mystery in which he had been a major player remained devoid of solution.

Finn rushed outside. But there was no sign of the killer. He had disappeared into the night like a fleeting wraith.

After they had reported the killing to the marshal, father and son retired to their room at the National Hotel. There was much to discuss.

'Looks like there's a heap more to this business than we thought, Finn,' Blake Dexter anxiously observed. He poured two generous slugs of brandy. 'Guess we need this after all the excitement.' Finn did not disagree. 'So what we gonna do about it?'

Finn's lean features assumed a determined cast. 'Nagle followed Matt out here. But why would anybody want him killed?'

'And how come Harper was on the same train?' wondered Blake.

'I've been thinking the same thing myself. No use speculating, though. The answer must lie in Kansas City.'

FIVE

EASTBOUND

The Dexters' questions were still hanging in the air when they left the room descending to the entrance lobby of their hotel. They were about to leave for Marny's Diner when a small boy approached them.

'Are you Mr Dexter?' the kid enquired.

'Which one do you have in mind?' Blake threw an amused look at his own offspring. 'Father or son?'

The kid shrugged. 'The guy who gave me this note just said to hand it to Dexter at the National Hotel. You two fellas fit the description.'

Finn's smile disappeared. 'Where did you meet this guy?' His voice was brittle and demanding.

The scruffy urchin picked up on the frosty mood. He stepped back nervously, ready to beat a hasty retreat.

'Out back in the alley,' he muttered. The kid was well used to painful backhanders from adults. 'I'm just the messenger. You want this note or not.'

Blake tossed the boy a quarter. It was caught with perfect dexterity and pocketed before the kid ran off.

When Blake read the brief message, his dark eyes glittered with anger.

'Take a look at this, Finn.'

His son was no less incensed by the contents. Slowly he read it out loud: *'Stick your nose in our business again and you'll end up like Nagle.'*

'What d'yuh reckon we should do?' Blake was worried.

His ashen features spoke more than any words could convey. His son could see that the older man figured they were getting out of their depth. Finn, on the other hand, was eager to press on. This was his big chance to prove himself as a true Pinkerton agent. He sat down in the lobby, a pensive frown puckering his handsome forehead as he worked out a plan of action.

'The only way to find out is for me to head for Kansas City,' he announced briskly. 'That seems to be where all the action is. We'll make a show of heading back to the ranch. Somebody is sure to be watching the hotel. That way the skunks will think we've given up.'

His eyes glittered as the plan unfolded. 'I'll return in the early hours and book a seat on the morning train. You stay at the ranch and keep a low profile. Keep an eye on Harper's movements and let me know if anything happens.'

'Sounds good,' replied his reanimated father. 'But you take care. You're my only kin and I want you back here in one piece. You hear?'

Finn gripped his father's hand. 'I'm a Pinkerton man

now, Pa. And you know what the boss says: *We always get our man!* And that's what I intend to do. But I'll make certain not to expose myself to needless danger.'

'I'll send Ned a wire to let him know you are coming,' Blake said. 'He'll be glad to put you up while you're there.' His next comment was edged with regret. 'Guess I'm too much of coward to tell him the truth about young Matt in a wire. Any chance that you could break the news?'

The deep emotion revealed in his father's glum features touched Finn to the core. He gripped his father firmly round the shoulders.

'I know you two are close. And you're right. It's best that I tell him what happened face to face. So don't worry. I'll make sure to handle it with kid gloves.'

A wan half-smile brightened the older man's countenance.

After paying their bill the two men left the hotel. Luck was with them in the form of the marshal. Hangdog Charlie Mancos had just returned from questioning the manager of the Jackdaw Hotel. The two riders made a point of informing the lawman that they were heading back to the Circle D.

It so happened that Spike Dobey was hidden in a doorway close by and heard the brief exchange. His warped features cracked in an ugly smirk. His stark warning had done the trick. He hung around to make certain the Dexters left town, then stubbed out his cigar and hurried away to relay the good tidings to his boss.

In the penthouse suite of the Prairie Oyster, Silas Harper was studying some papers when Dobey walked in. He was clutching a large cigar between his teeth.

'What kept you so long?' Harper snapped at the underling. 'All you had to do was pay off Cash Nagle and get back here.'

'It wasn't as simple as that,' the spy enunciated with vigour, bunching his fists. Dobey bowed to no man, least of all a pompous big shot. But he held his violent temper in check. 'A couple of snoops were tailing him. They knew he had something to do with Sullivan being gunned down.'

Dobey's defiant tone informed his paymaster that Spike Dobey was his own man and expected an equal measure of respect. Harper was well aware that the hard-boiled tough knew all about his scheming plans for victory in the forthcoming elections. He could not afford to upset the guy.

'All right, all right,' he muttered, injecting a note of appeasement into his voice. 'So what happened then?'

Dobey reached across the desk and helped himself to one of the senator's special brand of Havana cigars. He applied a match and drew in the unique flavour before satisfying the corpulent politician's barely contained impatience.

After Dobey had reported the recent events Harper relaxed.

'Nagle won't be needing this dough,' the undercover man grunted, handing over the payout, 'seeing as he's cashed in his chips.'

Harper ignored the witty observation. A frown cracked the politician's smooth brow. 'I'm still worried about those two interfering busybodies.'

'No need, boss,' Dobey assured him with a harsh guffaw. 'I put the frighteners on them. They sure got the message loud and clear. I saw them leave town myself.'

Harper guffawed too. This was good news.

'You keep the dough, Spike. Call it a bonus. You've done well. I can always use a man of your talents if'n you give me a call back in Kansas City. Guess you'll be catching the train in the morning, eh?'

Dobey pocketed the bonus. 'Guess so,' he drawled out, tapping the bulge in his jacket. 'But this will buy me a good send-off at Lulu Laverne's Hot House.'

Finn was one of the first passengers to board the east-bound the next morning. Another early bird was struggling to lift her valise on to the overhead rack. Ever the gallant gentleman, Finn hurried across.

'Let me help you, ma'am,' he offered, taking hold of a second bag perched on the lady's seat.

The young woman turned. Her face registered surprise. A pair of large brown eyes peered back at the handsome stranger. Limpid pools, they rested in an oval face that could have graced the pages of a society magazine. The good samaritan was transfixed. He just stood there, hypnotized, held in an irresistible trance, unable to move.

'Why, sir, that would be very kind of you,' the young woman replied. Her dulcet tones managed to break the trance.

Intent on settling herself in the carriage, she had failed to perceive the mesmeric effect she was having on the young man. Finn quickly pulled himself together and heaved the second piece of baggage next to its counterpart.

'Thank you very much for your help, kind sir,' purred the delectable creature, sitting down. 'I hope you don't mind if I take the window seat.'

Did he mind? What sort of question was that? This winsome dove had only intimated that Finn Dexter should join her for the upcoming journey. Teeth gleaming white as the mountain snow flashed an inducement that was not to be ignored. A busy little hat perched at an angle on her mass of auburn ringlets only served to enhance the vision of beauty in Finn Dexter's ogling peepers. Tipping his hat, he offered the girl a trembling hand.

'Finn Dexter, ma'am. Pleased to make your acquaintance. Are you travelling all the way to Kansas City?' The tremulous croak in his voice was concealed behind a brisk cough.

'Indeed I am, Mr Dexter,' she demurred indicating that he should be seated. The carriage was rapidly filling up with other passengers. 'My name is Candy Stockwell. And it is my good fortune that you happened along at the right time. A girl in my profession often attracts the wrong type of attention.'

Finn had come across that name some place before. His face crinkled in thought. The girl laughed at his discomfiture. 'You have doubtless seen my name on a poster outside the Blue Bell theatre. I'm a singer and have just finished a two-week stint there. And now I'm off to Kansas City for my next engagement.'

Finn's face reddened. 'Guess I ain't too acquainted with theatres. I've been away myself for some time.'

He remembered in time not to divulge the nature of his business in Kansas City, even to this winsome angel. Allan Pinkerton had always stressed the need for caution at all times when engaged on a job.

Everybody, no matter how innocent they appeared, should be regarded with suspicion until they had proved their good faith. Women were the most adept at worming information out of gullible dupes. No agent should ever allow his commonsense to be addled by a silky tongue, Pinkerton had adjured.

The advice was sound. A gila monster disguises itself as a simple hunk of rock before pouncing on its prey.

Finn moved the conversation on to general topics. Everybody else in the carriage faded to an indistinct blur in the company of Candy Stockwell. As a result Finn was totally unaware that he was being closely watched by a man who had entered the carriage and was standing by the door.

Spike Dobey was shocked to find the recipient of his blunt warning here on the train, bound for Kansas City. Of course, it could be a coincidence. But Dobey didn't believe in them. He soon convinced himself that Dexter's presence was no twist of fate. Shuffling down the aisle he asked if the seat adjacent to Finn was free.

'Sure thing, mister,' breezed Finn, barely according the newcomer a glance. 'Help yourself.'

Dobey sat down. As the train chugged eastwards his sceptical nature began to formulate the view that Dexter must know something. Maybe Cash Nagle had spilled something before he was taken out.

The train stopped to take on water at Salina Flatts. Finn left the train followed by Dobey, who saw him sending a wire. He sidled up as close as possible to the telegraph office as he could without arousing comment. Although unable to hear the full message repeated aloud by the telegrapher as he tapped the morse key, single words were picked up; *Kegan – doctor – bushwhacker.* Meaningless in themselves, they pointed to the reason why Nagle had been on the westbound train the previous day.

Dexter was clearly intent on uncovering the truth behind the shootings.

Returning to his seat on the train, Dobey knew what he had to do. His chance came on the long straight mid-way between the junction and Salina. The conductor came down the carriages asking for all able-bodied men to ready themselves for loading wood at the next halt.

On sections of the railroad system that crossed the treeless prairie land, contractors were employed to deposit logs at strategic points. This was to provide fuel for the insatiable locomotives' steam engine. It was an understood thing that male passengers helped with the task.

'Guess that includes you and me,' Dobey remarked to his travelling associate.

The two men removed their coats, rolled up their sleeves and joined the other men at the side of the train. Dependent on the number of such men, the loading could take anything up to an hour.

Dobey made sure that he and Finn worked side by side. He had not yet figured out how to engineer an 'accident' to take care of the nosy varmint. It was during the coffee and cookie break that the opportunity he had been angling for arose.

The guard asked for two men to go to the far side of the train where logs thrown on to the loco's tender had fallen off the far side. No wood could be wasted in such barren terrain.

'How about you and me, stranger?'

Dobey didn't wait for Finn to respond. He signalled to the guard that he had his volunteers. Finn shrugged. He was quite willing to go along with this friendly dude. It was no skin off his nose what job they did. The sooner a full complement of timber was loaded, the sooner they could be on their way, and, more important in his eyes, the sooner he could return to his probing of Candy Stockwell's plans for the future. Finn hoped that he might persuade the girl to include him in them.

The two men moved around the front of the chuffing and hissing locomotive. Dobey made sure that he was behind Finn as they picked up the logs. A quick look around to ensure they were alone, then he silently hefted a suitable bough and crept up behind the unsuspecting Pinkerton. The thick limb rose into the air.

Candy Stockwell chose that precise moment to lean out of the window. What she saw momentarily stunned her into immobility. Her eyes bulged in shock. Then, the stark nature of what was about to happen caused her to scream out a warning.

'Look out, Finn! Behind you!'

54

The intended victim twisted away from certain extinction just as Dobey swung the lethal bough at his head. Had it connected, Finn Dexter's head would have been shattered like an eggshell. The log hissed by, no more than an inch from its target. Finn fell to the ground but lashed out with his right foot. The blow was enough to force the would-be killer back.

Dobey cursed. Realizing that he had lost the initiative, his only thought now was to finish the job off quickly before the other members of the loading party appeared. His hand shifted to the small Colt Lightning hidden in his trousers pocket.

Finn grabbed up the fallen log and flung it at the upraised hand. The gun flew off and buried itself in a clump of grass, but not before it spat lead. The jolt was enough to turn the slug away from being a killing shot. It did, however, scythe through Finn's shirt into his arm. His face screwed up in a pained wince.

'You must be the dirty bushwhacker who tried gunning me down in the Jackdaw,' he snarled, scrambling away from the incensed Dobgey.

A manic gurgle of rage rumbled from Dobey's throat.

'You won't escape me a second time,' he growled.

Although unarmed, Dobey sensed that he now had the advantage and wasted no time in launching himself at Finn. His aim was to force the Pinkerton on to the track where the slowly moving train would finish the job he had started. Then he could claim it was an accident brought on by an argument over the guy's unwanted attention towards the lady.

With one arm *hors de combat*, Finn now found himself fighting for his life.

This jasper was a burly critter with muscles to spare. And, unlike Finn Dexter, he was uninjured. Dobey's warped face cracked in a mirthless grin of triumph.

'You ought never to have muscled in on the boss's affairs,' he grunted, trying to force his victim's head down on to the track. 'Anybody that does pays a heavy price.'

Finn saw the glint of pure evil reflected in the black eyes.

He tried pummelling the guy with his right hand, but lacked the strength. He was losing blood fast. And the rumbling loco was drawing ever closer. It sounded like an earthquake shaking the ground. Out the corner of his eye he could see the giant wheel no more than a couple of feet distant.

Was this the end of his lawman's career? Over before it had even got started.

Finn's good arm flopped to the ground. But a guardian angel was hard at work on his behalf. His flailing limb encountered the fallen bough. His scrabbling fingers immediately gripped the shaft. With one almighty effort he swung it at the brute's head. It missed, glancing off Dobey's shoulder, but it was enough to halt the murderous man's intent. That was all the help Finn needed.

His knee came up hard and solid into the midriff of his squirming adversary. Releasing the log, he grabbed the guy's hair. The pure instinct of survival kicked in, lending added strength to his exhausted muscles.

Another enormous hook of his leg sent the critter over his shoulder on to the railroad track.

Dobey's head hit the iron rail. Before he could recover his senses, the loco was on him. The scream of terror was cut short as the guy was decapitated.

Only then did the guard and the other passengers arrive to determine the cause of the gunfire. The engineer and his stoker had remained oblivious to the whole episode throughout. Candy Stockwell was the sole passenger privy to the bizarre occurrence. The sight of Spike Dobey's mangled corpse left her shaken and disturbed.

The train was held up for a further hour while Dobey's remains were put in to a bag and placed in the caboose. All the female passengers were kept well away while the grisly transfer was effected.

Finn was spared the unpleasant process on account of his injury.

Only later did one of the other passengers remark that he had seen the dead man before, some place.

'Where was it?' Finn pressed the man. 'This is important so that I can find out why he tried to kill me.'

The guy scratched his head, struggling to bring the recollection to mind. Then he snapped his fingers.

'I know!' he exclaimed. 'He was a faro dealer in Lew Jardine's gambling joint in Kansas City. They call it the Snake Eyes casino.'

'Much obliged.' That was all Finn needed to know. Now he had somewhere to start his search.

But first he needed to ensure that this gruesome incident had not deterred Candy Stockwell from continuing their burgeoning association. The girl was most concerned about his bullet wound. Much to his delight, she fussed over him like a mother hen while dressing the wound.

It was almost worth getting shot to have such enchanting attention.

SIX

WELCOME TO
KANSAS CITY

When the train finally pulled into the station at Kansas City evening was settling over the booming township.

By the year 1876, it had become the major stepping-off point for pioneers heading West. Along with St Joseph and Omaha to the north, it was a hub of activity. But Kansas City had become pre-eminent following the erection of the only bridge spanning the mighty Missouri River at that time. From then on its growth had been assured as a place where enterprising investors could make their mark.

The railroad was a major part of this burgeoning endeavour. Cattle pens surrounded the town. The lowing of thousands of steers awaiting shipment to the meat processing plants filled the air twenty-four hours a day.

The citizens soon got used to the constant noise. After all, it was the source of their prosperity.

But to a newcomer like Finn Dexter it provided something of a culture shock. Bewilderment at the hustle and bustle registered on his tanned face as he helped Candy and her baggage down on to the platform. People were hurrying hither and thither. This was nothing like the easy-going pace of life to which he was accustomed.

Candy picked up on the young man's bemusement.

'You'll soon get used to it,' she said as he helped her down from the train.

Somewhat discomfited by his tenderfoot manner, Finn quickly recovered his more nonchalant aplomb. He knew that he would have to be at the top of his game to match the sharp operators in a place like this.

'It was nice meeting you, Miss Stockwell,' he said, eager to delay the girl's departure. 'Perhaps we could meet up again sometime. The least I owe you is a fancy dinner for saving my life.'

The girl blushed. 'I'd like that very much, Mr Dexter.' The two acquaintances had not yet moved beyond the rather stilted phase of testing the water in their budding relationship. 'It's lucky that I happened to look out of the window just at that moment or. . . .'

Before either of them could make any further arrangements two men hurried across. One secured the girl's baggage while the other gripped her arm.

'The boss is mighty anxious for a word, Miss Candy, before your first performance. With the train arriving late, we ain't got a moment to lose.'

The speaker was a tough-looking jasper with a foreign accent that Finn adjudged to be German. He and his equally thuggish-looking associate urged the girl gently but insistently away from her new companion.

Ignoring Finn, they hustled the girl towards a covered brougham waiting outside the station. The suddenness of the incident caught them both by surprise. Before Finn realized what had happened, the horse-drawn carriage was disappearing towards the main part of the town.

Finn stood there, somewhat bewildered. Then it struck him that he had no idea where she was performing or staying. And Kansas City was a big place.

The station was situated on the outskirts of the city. Resigned to a long walk, he gathering up his carpetbag and headed in the direction taken by the brougham. He had only gone a few steps when he was approached by a man around his father's age. An altogether far more friendly character than those who had so abruptly spirited the delectable Miss Stockwell away.

'You must be Finn Dexter,' the man said, holding out his hand. Finn nodded accepting the proffered greeting. 'I'm Ned Sullivan. Glad you have come. Me and your pa go back a long way. He wired me that you were coming by train. But he didn't give anything away regarding your business in Kansas City.'

The older man was well dressed in a city suit. Grey hair peeped from beneath a fashionable silk-lined top hat. Bright blue eyes twinkled in welcome but there was a hint of sadness in them that could not be ignored.

'Although the circumstances are less than what I could have wished for with regard to Matt's situation,' Sullivan added.

'About your son, Uncle Ned. . . .' The councillor was not related, but Finn had always called him 'uncle' since he was a young boy. He had not seen the older man for some years, hence his not having recognized him.

Sullivan laughed, quickly interjecting: 'Reckon you're a mite old to be calling me that now. We're both men of the world, Finn. So plain old Ned will do just fine. Although when I get elected to Congress, I won't object to being called Senator.'

The two men laughed together, instantly comfortable in each other's company.

Finn was not given the opportunity of enlightening the older man of his son's fate as Sullivan ushered his guest over to a buggy. Once inside the carriage, Finn attempted to raise the tricky subject again. But Sullivan held up a hand.

'Let's get back to my house first. You must be tired after that long journey. We can discuss Matt's problems and your visit to our booming metropolis over dinner.'

The town councillor was a prosperous business man of integrity who lived in a large house in the most affluent suburb of the city. His campaign for state senator was supported by numerous organizations. Any smear on the candidate's reputation could easily derail the process.

That was the reason he had dispatched his wayward son to the Kansas outback. With Matt out of the way, it was hoped the campaign would run much more smoothly.

It was only when they reached Councillor Sullivan's house that the blood on Finn's coat became apparent.

'How did that happen?' said the worried councillor.

Finn apprised his host of recent events.

'I'll get my housekeeper to fix you up properly before dinner,' said Sullivan. 'She used to be a nurse before coming to work here.'

Following the meal prepared by the portly but efficient Mirabelle Flockhart, they retired to the smoking room. Finn had delayed mentioning the shooting of young Matt until they were alone.

The two men sat opposite one another, each occupying a wing-backed chair in front of a roaring log fire. Balloon glasses of French brandy and Havana cigars completed the relaxed ambience.

Finn then explained the disturbing circumstances connected with Senator Harper's visit to Ellsworth and Matt getting shot in the back. Sullivan listened intently without interruption. He then went on to explain that his son could be a bit wild at times.

'But he's a good kid and only needs some careful guidance to keep him on the right path. Seems like campaigning has taken up too much of my time of late. I've ignored the obvious signs. Matt liked gambling but always paid his debts. Then somebody took a shot at him.'

'Have you any notion as to why anyone would do that?' asked Finn, who was beginning to enjoy the luxury of city living.

Sullivan lifted his arms in bewilderment. 'Your guess is as good as mine, son. Maybe he got in with the wrong crowd. Who knows? But with the elections coming up I can't afford to have my name dragged through the dirt. That's why I sent him to stay with your pa.'

Finn's square jaw thrust forward. 'Did he ever visit a place called the Snake Eyes?' he asked hopefully.

'I don't rightly know where he got to.' Sullivan's face creased with bafflement. Then a look of condemnation brought a red tinge to the wrinkled visage. 'Although I sure hope he didn't frequent that den of iniquity.'

Finn's eyebrows lifted. 'Does it have a bad reputation, then?'

'Nothing the council have ever been able to prove. But rumours abound that some dubious practices go on at the tables.'

'Somebody must want Matt out of the way real bad, seeing as they sent two hired gunmen to finish the job.'

'Lucky you were on hand to square it else he would have been a goner for sure.' The older man's eyes watered. A few stray tears dribbled down his cheeks. He wiped them away, embarrassed at this undignified display of emotion from a supposedly resilient campaigner.

'I'd give up the whole idea of becoming a senator if'n it's going to put my boy's life in danger.'

'Well, I don't reckon it was a random act.' Finn's look hardened to a steely glint. 'And the answer to this mess lies in the Snake Eyes. So I need to get inside that dive to find out how it operates.'

Later on Ned rose from his seat intending to show

Finn to his room.

'Much obliged for the offer,' Finn said with a shake of his head. 'But I reckon it will be safer if'n I stay at a hotel. We don't know how this is going to end up. If Jardine links the two of us together, it could cause you trouble. And I sure don't want that.'

Ned saw the logic in that and reluctantly agreed.

'I'll drive you over to the Drexel Palace. A friend of mine owns it. He'll see you are made comfortable.'

They were heading towards the back of the house and the stable block when Ned paused in mid-stride.

'But if'n you are going to visit the Snake Eyes, you'll need some snappy duds. No offence, but range gear is out of the question. You wouldn't get past the doorman dressed like that.' They turned round and headed for the stairs. 'You're about Matt's build. Some of his clothes are sure to fit.'

Sullivan disappeared up the stairs and returned moments later with a selection of clothing draped over his arm.

'These should do fine.'

Later that evening, Finn was in his room at the Drexel. He had decided to take the bull by the horns and pay a visit to the gambling joint without delay. It was better to strike while the iron was still hot.

The clothes fitted perfectly. Topped off with a snazzy topper and silver-tipped cane, Finn moved across to a mirror to check himself out. The image that greeted his ogling peepers was not the Finn Dexter he knew. Facing him was a strutting dandy, a man about town. Someone he barely recognized.

'Who in tarnation are you, mister?' he blurted out.

It was like he had been transported to another world. This must be how the city gents dressed all the time. He felt like a tailor's dummy. This was not the way a profesional Pinkerton man ought to present himself. It was a side of life that was completely alien to the wild frontier territory into which he had been raised. But if this was the only means of gaining access to the high-swinging casino, then so be it.

The owner of the Drexel pointed Finn in the right direction for Snake Eyes. Ned Sullivan had not disclosed the reason for Finn's visit to Kansas City, merely stating that he was here on ranching business.

'You'll need plenty of dough in a place like that,' the hotel proprietor remarked.

That was no idle comment, as Finn observed on approaching the casino. It was clearly not a place frequented by the ordinary citizens, the common ruck. To one side was a parking lot for clients to leave their carriages. Numerous drivers were hovering about outside awaiting the return of their well-heeled employers. Their smart livery only served to enhance the atmosphere of success and plenty in this part of the city.

The large elegant building, complete with towers surmounted by golden spires, presented the image of a fairy castle. To the gullible, untrained eye was offered an image of dashing princes climbing its walls to rescue damsels in distress. To enter this fairytale land of pleasure necessitated mounting a broad flight of steps that led up to the grand foyer.

There the illusion terminated abruptly. Above the entrance was the name: *Snake Eyes,* mounted on a pair of giant dice, each showing the single spot which was presented as giant eyes fixed on those about to enter the casino. Finn could not help noting the ironic twist to the depiction: Snake Eyes luring the prosperous punters into parting with their hard-earned lucre contrasting with the Pinkerton 'Eye' making sure they were not cheated.

Beneath this lurid advert for games of chance stood two hard-boiled sentinels. Trying to appear efficient and professional they looked totally out of place in their tight penguin suits. Their purpose was clearly to block the entry of any undesirables.

The obsequious lackeys bowed to various ladies and gentlemen who were entering the premises. All were clad in their best finery: the men in black tuxedos, the ladies graceful and alluring in their shimmering gowns.

Finn was ushered in with barely a glance. He certainly looked the part and realized that he was wearing essential disguise for what he had in mind.

After handing in his hat and cane to the checkout girl, he asked the way to the gaming rooms.

'Straight ahead and through the arch, sir,' came the practised reply complete with the routine smile.

An easy-going pace was adopted with some degree of difficulty as he wandered towards the main playing area. Finn was eager to put his plan into action. But any hurried movement would have been decidedly out of place. He had to curb his impatience.

The ornate decor of the large room was something

to behold. It took his breath away. Crystal chandeliers hung from the ceiling. Oak panelled walls with ancient suits of armour at strategic points gave out an image of a noble and much esteemed ancestry.

Money spoke volumes here. And the dough clearly came from the suckers who gambled away huge fortunes on the various games of chance. Finn made a point of appearing casual as he circulated between the various tables. All the while he was searching for a dealer who, he figured, was on the take.

They were easy to spot if you knew what to look for. Finn was a pretty decent poker player and had come across most of the ruses practised by tinhorns. The first room was devoted to faro and appeared to be clean. So he moved effortlessly through a stylish archway into the next one.

Now this was more like it. Poker!

SEVEN

ROYAL COMEUPPANCE

Finn made a laid-back yet probing assessment of the numerous games being conducted. It wasn't long before he became suspicious of one particular jasper, who was giving out all the wrong vibes.

Finn paused, leaning against a column, glass of wine in hand. Observing the guy for a couple of games, he acknowledged that he was a pro when it came to sleight of hand. The trickster's dexterity was barely noticeable. Only someone who knew what to look for could have spotted the deft switch of cards.

But it had happened. A blink at the wrong moment and he would have missed it.

Finn waited for one of the losing players to throw in his hand and leave the table. Then he stepped forward and took the guy's place.

Rosco McGee was a typical cocky braggart. Confident of his ability to outfox these strutting peacocks, he soon became careless. His oversized velvet coat with its large sleeves held the key to the chicanery.

With glasses replenished and cigars lit, the new game commenced.

The first few hands proceeded with nothing untoward being attempted. McGee was sizing up the new mark, to judge his playing skill. Finn deliberately played the role of a witless popinjay to lull the tinhorn into a false sense of security. Everything proceeded in a normal fashion with little shift in fortunes among any of the players.

Then lo and behold, out the corner of his eye Finn saw the switch.

A rogue card had suddenly appeared in the gambler's hand. It must have been stuck up the sleeve of his coat. A frosty glint in his eyes and a slight lift of his right eyebrow was Finn's only reaction to something being amiss. None of the other players noticed the tension emanating from the newcomer. Finn assumed the classic poker-faced mien.

At the end of the hand, after the other players had pulled out, Finn continued to raise the stakes. Finally he called.

McGee stifled a scornful jeer as he laid his cards on the table.

'Sorry about this, buddy.' The dealer's feigned apology was as bogus as his hand. 'Full house, kings on eights beats your straight. The house wins.' An oily smirk pasted across the cheat's weasel-like features as he leaned across the green baize table to scoop up the pile of greenbacks.

Finn's hand shot out and gripped that of the card-sharp.

'Not so fast,' he rasped. 'You palmed that king of hearts, which means there has to be another in the main pack. Now you're going to deal them out face up to show these good folks the sort of cheating rat they've been playing with.'

The other players gathered round. None had the slightest notion that Rosco McGee had been playing them for fools. Eyes hard as granite fastened on to the gambler.

'You sure about this, mister?' asked an older man clad in the dress uniform of a cavalry major.

'Only one way to find out.' Finn's stony gaze held the crooked gambler in a snake eyes grip. 'Deal, tinhorn.'

But McGee was not surrendering that easily. 'You got this all wrong, mister. I'll have you thrown out for false accusations.' He called to one of the penguins who were patrolling the room. 'Hey, Max, we have a trou-blemaker over here.'

Max Steiner was a barrel-chested thug, short as he was broad. A mean face pinched by old knife scars was completely out of place in the refined setting. But he made an effective security man, which was why Jardine had hired him.

'What's this all about?' he rasped in a thick German accent.

'This rat has been cheating,' Finn growled out. 'All I want him to do is deal out the cards to show he palmed

71

that king of hearts. If I made a mistake, I'll apologize and leave.'

The strong-arm man knew all about McGee's sting, as indeed did Lew Jardine. A percentage of the tinhorn's underhanded take was paid to the house. So exposing the crook's cheating practices was not within the penguin's remit. Troublemakers were summarily dealt with. Steiner immediately laid a hand on Finn's arm.

'This way, mister. You're leaving now.'

That was a big mistake. Part of Finn's training with the Pinkerton organization was in unarmed combat, especially in a new method recently learned from a Japanese agent. Before he knew what had hit him, Steiner was flung across the card table, his right arm jammed up his back.

The bodyguard emitted a startled grunt of pain. 'Arrrrgh!' he howled. 'Let me go!' But Finn held on tight.

Rosco took that opportunity to draw a concealed derringer from his vest pocket. The small gun rose. But he was not quick enough.

'Look out, mister,' the cavalry major shouted. 'He's pulled a gun.'

With one hand firmly securing the minder's arm, Finn drew his own Colt Peacemaker. The gambler's small gun was barely out before he was staring down the barrel of the lethal .45. Rosco immediately recognized that he had been bested in the gunfighting stakes. A card manipulator rather than a gunslinger, he allowed the derringer to slip from his fingers. The major quickly snatched it up and stuck it in his own pocket.

Meanwhile, Lew Jardine was hosting a dinner party in a private room next door. The guest of honour was none other than Candy Stockwell. It so happened that the Snake Eyes was her next appointment. She had accepted the job as top of the bill after answering an advert in the *Kansas Tribune*.

Jardine was offering a much higher salary than she had previously been offered.

The casino boss was the archetypal debonair gent. Flowing dark-brown hair complemented an equally well-barbered moustache of the type currently in fashion. Pale blue eyes swept over his lovely companion. Subdued lighting accentuated a lean, angular face, giving Jardine something of a devilish air that had served him well in the seduction stakes.

He knew exactly how to treat a lady, the unspoken proviso being that they succumbed to his lecherous charms afterwards. Those who failed to surrender willingly were quickly replaced. Many ended up in one of the numerous bordellos around Kansas City, another of Jardine's sidelines.

He leaned in close and poured her a glass of finest French wine. His winning smile made her blush to the roots of her luxuriant Titian locks. Standing up he glided around behind and fastened a silver and diamond necklace around her swanlike neck.

'For you, my dear,' he cajoled. 'A token of my gratitude that you have chosen to work here at Snake Eyes.' He raised his glass in a toast. 'Let us hope that ours is a long and fruitful association.' What he omitted to say was that the bauble was only on loan until such time as he tired of her.

The gambler had started out at the bottom. His trade had been learned in the Kansas cowtown of Abilene before he had moved on to Wichita, where he had really made his mark. Not averse to bending the rules to suit his own ends, Jardine soon became a partner in his own saloon and gambling hall. Tinhorns like McGee were amateurs in the scurrilous game of card manipulation when compared to Lew Jardine.

Success had grown apace. Dealings in the meat processing business were also added to his growing list of successful ventures. It was inevitable that soon the rogue's ambitions would gravitate to Kansas City, where real money was to be gained.

The colonial mansion he now occupied had been purchased six months before at a knockdown price. One of his clients was a leading banker who had been persuaded that substantial gambling debts would not be good for business should they become public knowledge. The building had been transformed into the garish house of pleasure now known as Snake Eyes.

It was here that Candy Stockwell had arrived earlier that day. An innocent fly in the spider's web.

Jardine had given her a generous allowance to enhance her wardrobe. Such magnanimous gestures only served to make her feel that she had definitely made the right move in accepting the position. And the food was first class, prepared by a genuine French chef.

The gambler certainly knew how to make a girl feel on top of the world. He was a good ten years her senior, but she felt comfortable in his presence.

'After dinner you circulate around the rooms,' Jardine said, popping a succulent piece of braised pheasant into his mouth. 'Get to know the place and the clientele. You can make your debut tomorrow night.'

'This certainly is a step up the ladder for me, Mr Jardine—'

'Call me Lew,' the boss interjected. 'We're all friends here. And I hope that will be the case with you and me.' He kissed her hand; a lascivious gleam in his eye, held for a moment, was quickly replaced by a more businesslike regard.

'No riff-raff in any joint run by Lew Jardine. We only allow in those of high breeding' – a pause and a wry smile accompanied his next remark – 'who also have plenty of money to throw away.' Candy laughed along with him. After all, that was the reason she was here – to make a good living.

'That's why Snake Eyes is in business,' the oily flatterer continued. Then, reverting to a more serious tone, he added, 'But I run a clean operation. No cardsharps or underhanded practices. Anybody caught cheating is thrown out and told to keep away.'

The light conversation was abruptly interrupted much to Jardine's displeasure. Another hardcase, sporting the appropriate handle of Bull Maddox, bustled through the door without knocking.

'What do you want?' rapped Jardine, clearly irritated by the disturbance.

'We've got trouble in the poker room, boss. Better

come quick,' the burly tough ejaculated.

'What's happened?' demanded Jardine.

'McGee's been caught out.'

Jardine cursed.

'Dinner's over early, Candy. Time to earn your keep.' The genial host of moments before had changed brusquely into a ruthless operator. 'Get up on stage fast and keep these bozos occupied while I deal with this.'

Jardine threw back his chair and strode off with Bull Maddox, leaving Candy somewhat bewildered. At the door, he turned.

'What you waiting for, gal, Christmas?' The brusque reproof was totally at odds with the guy's previous charm. 'Do what you're paid for, and be damned quick about it.' Then he was gone.

So all that oily charm had been a veneer, false flattery. Candy sniffed. He was no better than any of the other lowlife deviants for whom she had worked.

Once in the poker room Jardine instantly picked up on the tense atmosphere. His probing gaze was drawn to a tall dude who was holding the dealer down over the table. It was obvious that he was no pushover: he was somebody to be reckoned with. He sped across to the table through a gap unceremoniously made by the penguins on duty.

'What goes on here?' the boss rapped out, effectively silencing the babble of conversation. It was the cavalry major who filled him in.

'This fella caught the house dealer trying to manipulate the cards. When he challenged the rat, McGee pulled a gun.'

Jardine knew about the crooked dealer's shifty tactics but had been prepared to connive with his skulduggery while the money flowed in. Now he displayed a suitable air of disgust that such deplorable practices had occurred on his premises.

The dealer was given no chance to deny the allegation. 'We do not tolerate any cheating at Snake Eyes. You're fired, McGee. Now get him out of my sight.'

Two penguins grabbed a hold of the dealer and frog-marched him to the door. But not before the tinhorn made a foreful remonstration.

'Hey Jardine!' he protested, struggling between his mean-assed guardians. 'What about my cut. We had a deal.'

At a curt signal from the boss McGee's outburst was hastily quashed with a well-aimed cosh. It was fortunate that in the furore, the meaning behind the crook's gripe was lost. Except, that was, to one man, whose suspicions were given an added boost. But Finn remained tight-lipped. He had no wish to put Jardine on the defensive.

'Please accept my profuse apologies, sir,' the casino proprietor gushed pasting on his most contrite expression. 'Come to my office now and you will be fully compensated.'

'Much obliged,' replied Finn.

To the rest of the assemblage, Jardine declared, 'Sorry about this, folks. There's always one rat who slips through the net. If'n you all step over to the bar, the drinks are on the house.'

That announcement provided a soothing balm in

the tight atmosphere. Free drinks always have that effect in any company, as Jardine well knew.

Jardine and his bodyguards, followed by Finn, passed through the main room where Candy Stockwell was now on stage performing a popular song of the day. A lively four-piece band accompanied her moving rendition. The audience were mesmerized by the lilting cadences of her voice.

As Finn passed the stage he glanced up.

The look of surprise plastered over his face was matched by that of the singer. But, ever the consummate professional, Candy never missed a note. The only outward sign of recognition was a widening of the eyes and a blanching of the cheeks. Otherwise her faultless performance continued with no hesitation at all.

'Good, ain't she,' commented Jardine as they passed.

'Sure is,' was Finn's burbled reply as he dragged his gaze away from the vision in green.

In the back office Jardine's ingratiating manner dissolved. After counting out the money Finn said he had lost, the boss thrust it into his hand.

'Here's your dough. Now leave. And don't come back.'

Finn made no move to obey the peremptory command.

'Not before I have my say.'

'What do you want?'

EIGHT

THE DIE IS CAST

'I hear tell you've been getting through a lot of dealers, Jardine. This place has a nasty smell about it that I intend to clean up. First there was that skunk you sent to Ellsworth to finish off Matt Sullivan. But he failed. And so did the back-up. Both of them are now pushing up the daisies.'

Jardine's back stiffened. His eyes narrowed to thin slits. A look of concern passed between the gambler and his bodyguard. At a slight twitch of his boss's head Maddox lurched across to grapple Finn to the ground. But he was too slow. The Pinkerton slewed to one side, ducking out of the scything bear hug. A solid right buried itself in the thug's stomach. Maddox doubled up gasping for breath.

'Your minders ain't much use either,' scoffed the Pinkerton man. 'I'd hire me some decent security in future.'

A second pile-driver with all his muscle behind it

finished the job. Bull Maddox went down in a sprawling heap. Before Jardine could grab the New Line .22 pocket revolver in his desk drawer, Finn had brought his own hardware to bear. The Peacemaker was cocked and ready for action.

Jardine's hand froze. 'Who in thunderation are you, mister? And what do you really want?' growled the braggart, sinking back into his chair.

'I'm a Pinkerton man here to find out who shot Matt Sullivan.' The announcement brought a startled look of shocked concern to the gambler's slippery features. A Pinkerton man! That was serious business. 'And I reckon you're involved.'

Although the news had momentarily stunned him, Jardine quickly assumed his customary bravado. He denied the whole thing.

'I have never heard of Sullivan. And you have no proof, not a shred of evidence to back up these wild allegations. I can have you in court for libel saying things like that about a respectable member of society.'

Finn couldn't resist a chortle.

'You're right, mister. I don't have any proof. But I intend to find it. And when I do, expect another visit, with the sheriff in tow.'

At that moment Max Steiner entered the room. He didn't see Finn who was hidden behind a hat stand.

'I see you got rid of that troublemaker, boss' he said. 'Maybe I should go after him and get the dough back in the usual way.' The first he knew of something being wrong was the splayed-out body of his associate on the floor.

'Shut up, you stupid clown,' snarled Jardine.

Finn, smiling, stepped into view.

'I might not have any proof of murder yet. But your gorilla here sure has a big mouth.'

Steiner was all set to make a blundering charge of his own. But the Peacemaker swung to cover him.

'I wouldn't if'n I was you, apeman. This gun makes no allowances for stupidity.'

Steiner might have been more brawn than brain but he was no fool. Finn knew when the chips were down. The bodyguard hunched down, ready to take advantage of any lack of concentration on his adversary's part.

The situation was getting a little too hot for Finn's liking. Another galoot could have heard the fracas and might cut him off at the back door. Nevertheless, the gun covering the two men was rock steady as Finn backed towards the rear door.

'I'm going now. But make no mistake, this isn't the last you've heard of this matter.'

He opened the door and fired a couple of shots at the two oil lamps illuminating the room. Both slugs shattered the glass, plunging the room into darkness. That was enough to give him some breathing space to get clear.

Jardine threw a few lurid curses after the retreating figure, then stumbled over to the inner door. There was a spare lamp in the corridor outside. No attempt was made to have Finn tailed.

He was not especially worried as he weighed up his options. There were various ways of discovering the rabble-rouser's whereabouts. The plethora of street urchins frequenting the alleyways of Kansas City would do anything for a half-dollar tip. He would soon know where the sidewinder was staying. He gave an order for Steiner to set the ball rolling.

'And get this lard bucket out of here,' he rapped, aiming a brutal kick at the rotund hulk that was Bull Maddox.

Furrows of thought ribbed his forehead. This Pinkerton menace had to be eradicated. Those guys were big trouble. Dogged and determined, they never gave up.

Once outside, Finn ran like the devil was on his tail, only pausing when clear of the immediate vicinity of the casino. He paused on a street corner, looking back. Thankfully nobody was in pursuit. And only Councillor Sullivan knew that he was staying at the Drexel Palace.

He had sure set the cat among the pigeons and no mistake.

Making his way along the unfamiliar streets, the one issue that stuck in his craw was a nagging worry that Miss Stockwell had unknowingly allowed herself to be duped by the double-dealing critter. Why was a girl of her ilk working for a scumbag like Lew Jardine?

Then another, more pressing issue raised its ugly head. The meandering route for which he had opted had thrown off any pursuit. But now Finn was lost. And his arm was aching. The fracas at Snake Eyes had shifted the bandage on his arm and restarted the bleeding. The sooner he reached the hotel the better.

But at night all the streets in this unfamiliar town looked the same. His salvation came in the form of a street kid who led him back to the Drexel, for a fee of course, which the greenhorn visitor was more than happy to pay.

And therein lay his folly.

Street kids survived amidst the squalor on the far side of the railroad tracks where saloons, honky-tonks, low dives and brothels offered all-day entertainment to the lower level of Kansas City society.

They came into the more respectable areas, searching for naive marks like Finn Dexter. An underground grapevine system of communication had proved very successful. It was also highly remunerative for their leader, a sly rooster called Slickfingers Guthrie. His responsibility was to report any strange occurrences to Jardine on a regular basis.

The routine was a small price to pay for keeping the gaming boss up to date with what was happening in the city. It was a little after midnight when Slickfingers knocked on the back door of Jardine's office.

'Come in,' came the muted grunt from the far side. The devious runt sidled in. His shifty eyes flickered back and forth. Jardine knew who it was without looking up from his accounts. He wrinkled his snout at the unpleasant odour now enveloping the room.

'Anything to report?' he rapped out. The devious little dwarf shuffled his feet.

'Seems like one of my kids took a well-dressed dude back to his hotel,' Slickfingers piped up in that characteristic high-pitched warble that set the gambler's teeth on edge. 'The kid would have thought nothing of it, but this fella had blood all over one sleeve of his coat. And he wasn't wearing a hat.'

Jardine looked up. This was interesting. Blood, coupled with a hatless dandy. This latter point alone would have merited attention. No gentlemen would step out bare-headed. It just wasn't done.

'The guy told the kid he was fresh in town and had been to a casino.'

'Did he say which one?' The gambler's eyes gleamed.

'No. But he was coming from this direction.'

The gang boss nodded. It had to be that troublesome Pinkerton.

'So which hotel is he staying at?'

'The Drexel Palace.'

'You done well, Slickfingers.' Jardine opened his billfold and peeled off some notes. 'And make sure you don't spend it all in the same saloon.' A snappy gesture indicated that the meeting was over.

The fawning lackey scurried over to the door. Then he turned.

'Any chance of me getting a job here, boss?' he enquired hopefully.

'Not at the moment, but I'll keep you in mind when a vacancy occurs. Now git!' In fact, Slickfingers Guthrie was the last person he would want waiting upon the needs of his clientele. As soon as the kindergarten overseer had departed, Jardine shouted for Max Steiner to join him.

Meanwhile, Candy Stockwell had just finished her act to rapturous applause. She hurried off stage,

84

anxious to find out what Finn Dexter was doing at Snake Eyes. It had been a shock to see her fellow rail passenger here.

She asked a passing waiter where he had gone.

'Last I saw, miss, he was with the boss. They were headed for his office. I heard there was some trouble in the poker room.'

The man then hurried off about his duties.

Candy made her way towards the rear of the casino where Jardine had so recently been entertaining her. The door of the office was slightly ajar. The subdued murmur of voices could be heard through the small gap. She edged closer, hoping to earwig what was under discussion.

'That bastard is a thorn in our side, Max. I want him removed, permanently.' Jardine's tone was hard as granite. 'So far he has no proof that I had Matt Sullivan shot. But we can't take any chances with the job we have planned and Harper running for re-election.'

'Don't worry, boss,' the underling growled out in a thick German accent. 'I know just the guy to do a clean job. They call him Panther Jack.'

Jardine threw him a quizzical frown.

'And like his namesake,' the bodyguard went on, 'he is stealthy and quiet as the grave, yet deadly when riled. His weapon of choice is a ten inch Bowie knife. Sneaking into a hotel bedroom will be chickenfeed to him.'

'But can we trust this feline visitor to keep his mouth shut?' The boss did not like hiring outside help. He preferred his own men to do any dirty work.

'Me and Panther go back a-ways,' Steiner informed his boss. 'We worked together in Leavenworth and Topeka before coming here. I organized the jobs and he slipped in and pulled the goods. We only split up when I came to work for you. But we still keep in touch. He's your man, boss. I guarantee it.'

That fervent declaration satisfied Jardine. 'OK, Max, you see to it. He's staying at the Drexel Palace.'

'At this time of night Jack will be propping up the bar in the Round House saloon on Emporia Street. I'll go down there straightaway. Our man ought to be fast asleep by then. The early morning hours are the best time for Panther Jack to strike.'

Steiner accepted a cigar from his boss and they both lit up. Smoke drifted through the open door.

Candy was about to back off when the door was flung open and the two men emerged. Jardine was startled to see the new singer there. Knowing that her own survival was in the balance, the singer didn't hesitate to take the initiative. Her skill at handling difficult audiences now came into play.

Before the casino boss could challenge her presence there and maybe conclude that she might have heard something, Candy quickly got in first.

'It's about that piano player in the band, Lew. He can't—'

'Not now, Candy, I'm busy. See me about it later,' he butted in, hurrying past.

The girl emitted a sigh of relief. Thankfully, he had not the slightest suspicion that she had been listening at the door. His mind was clearly on the business of getting rid of that troublemaker.

Although no name had been mentioned, she had little doubt that the man in question was Finn Dexter. Candy was shaking with nerves. She had worked in some shady joints, but nothing where murder had been involved. What should she do?

Finn was in mortal danger. And she had the means to alert him to the deadly peril he was facing. He had to be warned without delay.

With her act over for the night, Candy was free to do her own thing. Returning to her room, she donned a bonnet and shawl. She slipped quietly down the back stairs and let herself out into the warm night air. A gentle breeze shifted the leaves of the nearby stand of cottonwoods. An owl hooted mournfully in the distance.

After a quick glance around to ensure she had not been spotted the girl headed for the nearest rank of hansom cabs waiting on the street corner. She directed the driver to take her to the Drexel Palace. After alighting from the cab Candy hurried inside the hotel. Then she realized that she had no idea of Finn Dexter's room number.

Luckily a night receptionist was on duty.

Candy sucked in her cheeks. She knew exactly how to handle snooty hotel clerks. An extra thick application of rouge was applied to her tempting lips. The velvet bonnet was adjusted to a more jaunty angle. With plenty of cleavage on show, the image Candy wished to depict was contrived. She sauntered into the entrance lobby of the Drexel Palace. With lowered gaze and husky voice, she enquired for Mr Dexter's room number.

'He expecting company then?' asked the smirking clerk. 'The guy didn't strike me as the type who paid for his pleasures.'

Candy hitched up her bosom provocatively. Inwardly seething at the leering clown's assumption, she was nevertheless pleased that her subterfuge was succeeding.

'We have an . . . erm . . . arrangement. It was sorted out in advance with my employer.'

The clerk's eyes were glued to the girl's ample front window. His head gestured towards the flight of stairs leading to the upper floors.

'Room number nine, second floor,' he burbled.

'Much obliged, honey,' purred Candy. 'Maybe I'll see you around sometime.' A sly wink and she was heading for the stairs.

Room number nine was at the end of the corridor. A brisk tap on the door was repeated when nobody answered. Then a voice blurry with sleep answered from the other side.

'Who's there?'

'It's me, Mr Dexter, Candy Stockwell. We met on the train. I need to speak with you urgently.' The girl's hushed yet clearly alarmed tone shook the somnambulist from his lethargic torpor.

He threw open the door and quickly peered down the corridor to ensure nobody was watching. He gave a snappy gesture, uttered a brisk 'Come in!' and the girl was inside the room.

Finn was wearing a dressing-gown supplied by the

hotel on top of his nightshirt. His hair was dishevelled but he was still the dashingly handsome man she recalled. Without any preamble she launched into a garbled account of the recent events she had over-heard. She was breathing hard and was clearly distressed, the jumbled facts became intermingled with woebegone flights of fancy. Tears welled in her eyes.

Finn gripped her shoulders.

'Easy there, Miss Stockwell, you're safe here with me,' he whispered leading her over to a sofa. He sat the trembling girl down and poured out a glass of brandy. 'Now drink this slowly and let's have it again. And this time, stick to the facts in a way I can understand.'

When she had finished Finn stood up and paced the room. It was obvious that neither of them was safe here if what she had said about this Panther Jack villain was correct. And he had no reason to doubt her version of events.

Pouring himself a generous slug of brandy, he slung it down in a single gulp. The fiery tipple barely touched the sides of his throat. But it did help to focus his mind on how to deal with this perilous situation.

'The main thing now is to ensure you are not mixed up in this mess.'

'Oh Finn, Finn,' she wailed, clutching at the lapels of his dressing-gown. The normal decorum regarding name etiquette had dissolved in the trauma of their perilous situation. 'You must be very careful. Jardine is a dangerous man. I would never have gone to work for him if . . .'

Finn placed a finger across the girl's mouth stilling

89

any further outpouring. Her pouting lips were poised inches from his downturned face. Without any prompting he bent down and kissed her. Her response was fervent and immediate. Caught in a mesmeric swath of passion, their bodies moulded into a hot embrace.

At last they surfaced. Breath came in staccato gasps. Both of them were stunned as to what had actually just taken place. Yet neither felt any embarrassment. It had been the natural reaction of two people suddenly realizing their undeniable commitment.

But the reality of their hazardous circumstances still remained as stark as ever.

'You must get back to Snake Eyes,' Finn urged. 'Be careful to avoid being seen. There is no reason for Jardine to suspect you are involved in any way. Just continue with your regular routine and let me handle this in my own way.'

He went on to give her a concise account of his reason for coming to Kansas City. Allan Pinkerton's warning about disclosing information was disregarded. Love is blind where a beautiful woman is involved.

The fact that he was a Pinkerton agent only served to make Candy more concerned for his safety. After slipping on some proper clothes, he led her down the back stairs and hailed a cab to take her back to the casino.

They clasped hands through the cab's open window.

'You take care now,' the girl cautioned. 'I'd hate to lose you now that we've become more than passing acquaintances.' The cool light cast by a streetlamp lit up her face.

'No need to worry about me, Candy,' Finn replied,

squeezing her hand. 'We Pinkertons know how to handle ourselves.' He stepped back as the cab lurched into motion. In truth, he had no idea how this was going to pan out. The immediate problem was how to deal with the threat to which Candy had alerted him.

Finn had no idea when the killer would show. All he could do was make adequate preparations. Then wait.

NINE

NIGHT PROWLER

Back in his room, he arranged the sheets and blankets to look as if there was a sleeping occupant in the bed. With only the soft radiance of a streetlamp filtering through the window, the shadowy form was good enough to fool all but the most sceptical intruder.

He then settled down in a chair behind the door to await the night prowler.

Time passed slowly. He soon adjusted his perception to the normal creaks and groans of a building at rest. The occasional dog barked. A late-night reveller staggered by outside, warbling a timeless ditty. Nothing suspicious or out of the ordinary.

An ethereal glow cast by the half-moon cast soft shadows in the dark room. Disturbingly strange shapes assumed by the furniture could have unnerved a less stoic watcher. Although nervous regarding the forthcoming confrontation, Finn was eager to tackle the varmint. The more he considered the problem, the angrier he became, especially towards the miscreant who was responsible, namely Lew Jardine.

That hostility sharpened his resolve to bring the culprit to justice.

But remaining alert following such an eventful day was difficult. Finn's head drooped on to his chest. He would have fallen asleep had not the gun he was holding slipped out of his hand. The dull thud on the piece of carpet brought him instantly awake. He stood up, doused his face in cold water and resumed his watch.

Only moments later a distinctively alien sound impinged upon his newly alerted senses.

It was only a slight scratching noise over by the window as the catch was eased back. There followed a moment of hesitation as the intruder waited to ensure his attempted entry had passed unnoticed by the room's supposedly slumbering occupant. A faint rattle followed as the sash window rose slowly on his hangers.

Finn tensed, his hand gripping the revolver. The dark silhouette of a hunched figure appeared against the dim light as the curtains were pushed aside. A leg appeared through the gap as Panther Jack stepped lithely into the room. He paused to take stock, then slid into the dim shadows to get his bearings and allow his eyes to adjust.

An arm was raised as he cat-footed across to the bed. The light glinted on the steel blade clutched in his right hand. Not a sound was made. The killing arm descended, once, twice, three times. But it soon became clear to Panther Jack that he had been duped. This was no solid human form he was stabbing. It was too darned soft.

He cursed.

That was when Finn made his presence felt.

'Drop the knife, mister,' he snarled. 'I've got you covered. One false move and this gun does all the talking.'

But the Panther had not earned his name without good cause. The knife was immediately flicked towards the sound of the challenging command. In the dusky gloom it missed its intended target but pinned Finn's coat sleeve to the wall. That was enough for the prowler to leap on to his adversary.

Desperation to release his arm lent Finn added strength. A rending tear and he broke free.

The two combatants rolled over on the floor. Cursing and grunting, each of them strove to gain that vital advantage. Fists flew but none secured the telling blow that was needed. Finn managed to throw his much lighter opponent away. Both scrambled to their feet, circling each other warily. Finn contrived a lunge at his opponent. As the Panther side-stepped, his good arm circled the little rat's lean frame dragging him over.

'Who sent you, mister?' Finn snarled.

The Panther hawked out a brittle guffaw. 'Somebody who reckons you're poking your nose where it ain't wanted.'

The strained reply hissed out as he struggled to gain the upper hand. Finn held him tight. But the wily critter was more used to this form of combat than was

Finn Dexter. It was like grappling with a slippery eel. Somehow, the Panther managed to wriggle out of the Pinkerton's arms. A firm jolt in the chest caused Finn to trip over a chair.

The killer stepped back, producing a second knife from the back of his belt.

'Nobody can beat the Panther at his own game,' rapped the slimy toad. A warped smile cracked his twisted visage as he waved the lethal stiletto, then struck down at his victim, 'least of all some hayseed from up country.'

Finn didn't bother to reply. His whole being was concentrated on surviving the rat's deadly thrust. Realization of how much he had sadly underestimated not only the wily Panther's deadly proficiency but also his own weakened state, had come too late. As the knife descended, he swung to one side. The blade scythed past, a mere whisker away from burying itself in his neck.

As he scrambled crablike sideways, his hand lit upon the fallen revolver. He swung the gun to cover Panther Jack.

'Hold it!' Finn shouted, still anxious to avoid killing the assassin. But the guy had no such scruples. Killing was in his blood and he was not going to be denied now. Uttering a frenzied howl, he snatched up the fallen knife and hurled himself at the fallen man.

The gun exploded. The flash of igniting powder lit up the room. A scream rent the air as the heavy .45 hunk of lead smashed into the Panther's chest. Smoke filled the room along with the acrid stench of burnt cordite.

Panther Jack was dead. Finn Dexter rolled away from the still form, sucking air into his heaving lungs. That had been a close call and no mistake. Then his arm began to ache something terrible.

The patter of running feet along the corridor outside told him that the racket had not gone unreported. A sharp rap on the door was immediately followed by a curt demand for entry.

'What is going on there?'

It was the panic-stricken voice of the night clerk.

'Open up immediately, or the sheriff will be informed.'

Finn stumbled to his feet and unlocked the door. The smoking gun was still gripped in his hand. The clerk gulped, stepping back a pace and raising his hands.

Finn quickly discarded the pistol.

'Don't worry, I ain't gonna shoot. But you do need to send for the sheriff. A man just broke into my room and tried to kill me.' He jerked a thumb over his shoulder. 'He's in here now. And he won't be leaving except in a pine box.'

Other hotel guests had emerged from their rooms. Fearful mutterings echoed down the corridor.

'Nothing to worry about, folks,' the clerk said, reassuring them that the fracas was over and being dealt with. He had clearly dealt with such emergencies before. 'Just an accident with a loaded pistol. Now if you would all return to your rooms, I'll have some coffee and cookies sent up.'

That appeared to satisfy everyone.

96

Not somebody who was prone to panicking in tough situations, Finn quickly took stock of his options. Jardine would be waiting for his hired killer to report the success of his mission. Finn intended to take the guy's place.

After Panther Jack's body had been removed Sheriff Bill Moody arrived. Finn spun him a tale that it must have been a random break-in. The intruder had forced the window and tried to knife him when disturbed. Finn had been forced to shoot him in self-defence. He had no wish to have the local starpacker breathing down his neck when he confronted Lew Jardine the next day.

That explanation appeared to satisfy the sheriff. If Finn had admitted the truth to himself, he wanted to complete his mission without any help from the official law authorities in order to impress his boss. Only at the final hurdle would the sheriff be called in to tie up the loose ends.

That was the intention. But the most stringently calculated plans had a nasty habit of slapping you in the face. On such occasions the experienced Pinkerton detective proved his mettle. Finn Dexter was still only a novice. Had he the acumen to pull this off against inveterate villains like Lew Jardine?

There was only one way to find out.

But first he needed the professional attention of a sawbones. The manager of the Drexel Palace dispatched a porter to summon his own medic who expertly cleaned and stitched the bullet wound.

The rest of the night passed in a blur. With the help

of a prescribed sedative, Finn enjoyed an unbroken sleep for the rest of the night. He was awakened by milk carts and night-soil men passing by outside as the city opened its doors to the new day.

Next morning he discarded the smart tuxedo of the previous night reverting to the range gear he much preferred: a grey flannel shirt beneath a tan leather vest and corduroy trousers stuck into high-sided riding-boots. All topped off with the trusty old black Stetson. After strapping on his tooled leather gunbelt he felt better already.

Those fancy duds were not really his thing.

Palming the ivory-handled Colt Peacemaker, he twirled the chamber across his arm checking to ensure the gun was fully loaded. A deft flick on the middle finger and the revolver settled back into its holster.

Finn Dexter was now ready to make his move.

Morning was not the time when many people were about in the vicinity of Snake Eyes. He skipped up the back stairs and slipped silently in through the rear door. The corridor was empty. He moved stealthily down towards Jardine's office, where he paused to listen. The muted hum of voices penetrated the thin wood.

Finn was at the point of no return. He could turn away now, retreat and pass all the information he possessed over to the law.

The trouble was that he had no solid proof that Jardine, or indeed Silas Harper, were involved in the various criminal rackets and political chicanery. It was all just speculation. The skunks could deny everything.

It was his word against those of so-called respectable businessmen. The sheriff could do nothing and Finn Dexter would be humiliated.

His rap on the door was answered by a brisk order to enter.

Jardine rose to greet his visitor, whom he was assuming to be Panther Jack, reporting on the success of his mission. The gambling boss was dishevelled. Rumpled clothes and hair askew indicated that he had been up all night awaiting the killer's arrival. A far cry from the urbane boaster of the night before. A look of stunned surprise greeted the visitor.

'W-what are y-you doing here?' Jardine stuttered. 'I thought—'

'I know who you were expecting, Jardine,' Finn snarled, drawing his revolver to cover the shifty gambler and his bodyguard. 'The rat you sent to finish me off ain't coming. He's at the undertaker's, being measured up for a pine overcoat.'

The hunted look in Jardine's shifty gaze told Finn all he needed to know. He then went on to deliver the statement that he hoped would uncover the braggart's guilt once and for all.

'He's just like the other hired killers you sent to Ellsworth. They both failed. Neither of them could make a good job of finishing off Matt Sullivan. And now they're strumming the devil's tune.'

'What do you mean?' The gambler's face was ashen, his regard wary. 'I don't know what the heck you are talking about.'

Finn smiled. But it emerged as a hard, mirthless leer.

'Oh yes you do. Matt Sullivan is still alive,' he snarled. 'That backshooter on the train struck him down all right. But he didn't kill him.'

'That's a damned lie! Don't believe him, boss!' The denial was blurted out by Max Steiner. 'Spike Dobey sent a wire saying the doc told him the kid was dead.'

'Shut up, you durned fool!' rasped Jardine. But it was too late. Finn now had the truth. Lew Jardine had indeed dispatched the two killers to Ellsworth: the second to finish the job the first had failed to complete in Kansas City.

'That was a story we put around to fool you.' Finn gave a harsh chortle. 'And it worked a treat. Truth is, Matt is going to survive and is ready to testify in a court of law all about what he saw and heard.'

This last thrust hit home with a vengeance. Both of the crooks were so hyped up, knowing that their cover had been blown, that they were willing to try anything to stop this interfering troublemaker bringing in the law. Their hands hovered menacingly above their holstered gun butts.

'Don't try it, either of you,' Finn growled. 'I'm going. And this time, I'll make darned sure nobody follows. Now, turn around.' The two crooks hesitated, each assessing whether they could get the better of the man holding the gun.

'Turn around, I said!' came the steely command. Looking down the business end of the Peacemaker's squat barrel was enough to force the malefactors to obey.

Finn backed to the door and removed the key. Once

outside he locked the door. It was only a temporary measure, but enough to allow him to get clear.

But Finn did not venture far.

Hidden deep in the shadows, he waited for Jardine to leave the casino. Five minutes later the door opened and the gambling boss slipped out. This was what Finn had hoped would occur. Once the touch paper had been ignited, he knew that the varmint would need to inform the big boss.

Now all he had to do was follow at a safe distance and see where he went.

Jardine was so intent on reaching his destination that he gave no heed to the notion that he might be tailed. He headed uptown towards the wealthy locality where Councillor Sullivan also had his residence.

At the end of the tree-lined avenue Jardine halted. This time he did pause to look around. But Finn was well concealed behind a wall. Satisfied that he was alone, the gambler pushed open a large iron gate and hurried up the driveway to the front door. After rapping hard he was admitted by a flunkey.

Finn knew that venturing closer would be imprudent. Any attempt to break in would be pushing his luck too far. Whoever lived here would certainly be known to Ned Sullivan. Finn was pretty darned sure who that would be. He hurried along the avenue to the Sullivan household.

There he was invited in. The councillor was having breakfast and insisted that Finn should join him. Over coffee the Pinkerton related the events that had befallen him since leaving the previous night. Sullivan was shocked.

'You're right that Silas Harper lives in that house,' said Sullivan, sipping his cup of coffee. 'Matt must have uncovered some of their underhand dealings. Knowing him as I do, it's more than likely he threatened to spill the beans unless they paid him to keep his mouth shut.'

Finn then revealed his suppositions. 'When he went to collect the dough, one of Jardine's stooges must have been waiting to gun him down. But the gunman made a mess of it. Didn't he tell you why he'd been shot?' Finn asked the councillor.

'All he would say was that some guy owed him money and pulled a gun when Matt called in the debt. He said he would sort it out in his own good time. I didn't believe him but there was nothing more I could do. That was when I decided to contact your pa and send the boy out to Ellsworth for spell.'

'Jardine must have had your place watched so that he could follow Matt when he left. It just so happened that Harper was on the same train along with his hired gunman. Lucky for him but bad for Matt,' Finn surmised.

Sullivan stood up and paced the room. His face had assumed a worried aspect.

'Trouble is, we have no proof that Harper is running things. He's a clever cuss who always covers his tracks. We need firm evidence if'n he's going to be caught out.'

Finn had been listening. He carefully set down his coffee cup and gave the councillor a craggy look of determination.

'Reckon I have an idea how we can draw him out—'

Sullivan butted in nervously. 'You ain't going back to Snake Eyes, are you Finn? That skunk Jardine will have all his goons on watch. First sight of you and they'll shoot you down.'

Finn raised his hands to calm the worried man. 'I sure ain't that green, Ned. There's another way I can get inside without being spotted.' His eyes were gleaming with anticipation. 'If'n this goes according to plan then Harper will be all washed up.'

He then went on to outline what he had in mind.

TEN

A SWEETENER FROM CANDY

Ned Sullivan arranged for one of his most trusted employees to deliver the letter addressed to Miss Candy Stockwell at the Snake Eyes Casino. Thereafter he was to deliver another to the sheriff. The lawman was asked to be at the rear of Snake Eyes at an appointed hour and to bring his cuffs along.

The singer was in her dressing room when a knock came on the door.

'Come in,' she called out while applying the thick make-up needed for stage performances. Unlike many other places in which she had performed, Snake Eyes allotted its star act a personal dressing room.

'Letter for you, Miss Candy.'

She thanked the young stage hand who delivered it. A quizzical frown hardened the soft contours of her silky features. Who could be sending her letters at this time of the day? She was preparing for a matinée performance after lunch. Perhaps it was from an admirer. Although the only person towards whom she felt any affection had purposely placed his life in perilous danger.

Ever since she had left Finn at the Drexel Palace, Candy had been fretting constantly that news of his violent death would reach her. The kisses and tender moments they had shared were brief and fleeting. But they had changed her life. She couldn't get the young Pinkerton detective out of her mind. The very thought of his touch on her skin sent shivers down her spine.

Yet ever the consummate performer, she had striven to put aside her concerns for his safety. The show must go on. Anything else and Jardine might cotton on to her anxiety and draw his own warped conclusions. So here she was, preparing for the next performance. She turned the letter over in her delicate hands.

Was this some bizarre means of informing her that the fear in her heart had become a gruesome reality? There was only one way to find out.

After turning the letter over once again, she opened the envelope and extracted the sheet of paper. It was from Finn. She breathed a deep sigh of relief from between gritted teeth. Quickly she perused the contents.

It turned out that Jardine had admitted his part in the shooting of Matt Sullivan. But it was only Finn's word against his. Absolute proof of his guilt and association with Senator Harper's nefarious affairs was required. And that was where Candy's help would be vital.

Finn then set out exactly what he wanted her to do.

The next show was not due to commence for another half-hour. That was enough time for her to put in place the first part of the plan. It was a nerve-racking moment for the young singer. Should her part in the ploy be discovered, Jardine's reaction would be ruthless and terminal. Finn was well aware of this and had assured her in the letter that he would readily under-stand if she decided to back out.

No such refusal was even considered. Finn needed her help to thwart these lawless brigands, and she would give it wholeheartedly.

Candy was well aware that ever since Finn Dexter's visits to the casino Jardine had posted guards on every entrance. What she did not know was that they had been ordered to shoot him on sight.

She opened the door of her room and peered out. Thankfully, at this time of day nobody was around. Moving cautiously, she made her way round towards the main showroom. At the end of the corridor was a door leading to the back alley where Finn was waiting.

Bull Maddox was leaning against the wall, picking at his nails with a knife. A large purple bruise covered half his ugly mush. The plan involved somehow removing Maddox so that Finn could be admitted. He had left that up to her.

Candy suppresed a half-smile full of guile as she sashayed up to the lolling sentinel.

'Some'n I can do for you, miss?' warbled Maddox,

drawing himself up to his full height. A leery grin creased his pockmarked face. His ragged moustache twitched. He rubbed his palms over his locks of greasy black hair in a feeble attempt to smarten himself up.

Candy almost laughed aloud. Stifling a derisive snort, she casually brushed an imaginary speck of dirt from his jacket lapel as she leaned in close. Her exotic perfume couldn't fail to arouse the bumbling thug. Maddox reddened as Candy flicked her long eyelashes suggestively.

'Seems that I've left my purse in the dressing room, Bull,' she murmured in his ear. 'You couldn't nip back and get it for me, could you?' This last entreaty was uttered in her huskiest drawl.

'I-I ain't sure, Miss Candy,' burbled the hapless guardian. 'The boss says I ain't supposed to move from this spot.'

Candy sidled in closer. Her hand toyed with the tough's necktie.

'All my personal stuff is in there. A girl can't be too careful now, can she?'

Maddox just stared at her heaving cleavage, totally lost for words.

'I'd be ever so grateful,' she purred. That did it. Those big round eyes melted the hulking tough's resolve.

'OK,' he muttered, gulping in astonishment at this new singer making eyes at him. Nothing like this had ever happened to Bull Maddox before. Any liaisons in that department had been serviced by the calico queens at the boss's cathouses. 'I'll do it just for you. Stay here.

I won't be long.'

Candy had made sure that the purse was not openly on view in order that the guard would need to search for it. That would give her and Finn more time to arrange the next part of the scheme.

Once Maddox had disappeared round the corner Candy wasted no time in unlocking the outside door. Finn quickly slid through into the plush corridor, his trusty Colt gripped firmly in his right hand.

The pair embraced quickly. But with Bull Maddox on the prod there was no time for anything more than a brief peck.

'Thanks a bunch, Candy. I sure am grateful for your help,' he gushed, holding her close. 'But I wouldn't have thought any less of you if'n you had refused to back my play.'

The girl brushed off the remark.

'What you are doing is the right thing,' she emphasized while ushering him down the corridor towards Jardine's office. 'I've only been here two days and already the rumours of Jardine's dubious dealings are the talk of the casino. Nobody wants to buck the system for fear of being rubbed out. It's happened on two previous occasions according to one of the dancers. And it's likely the card-sharp you flushed out will be found floating face down in the Missouri River.'

A door banged somewhere else in the building. The unexpected jar startled them both.

'We have to hurry!' she urged, leading the way. 'That lump Maddox will be back soon.'

Outside the office door Finn handed Candy another

letter, with brief instructions for its delivery. A quick brush of lips and she was ready to carry out another crucial role that they had discussed on the short walk down the corridor. The two locked eyes. Then Finn gave a curt nod and she knocked on the door. Without waiting for a reply she called out,

'It's Candy, boss. You asked everyone to keep a lookout for that troublemaker. Well, I've seen him.'

A brisk exchange of words inside the room indicated that the news had caused a stir. The noise of scraping chairs was followed by the hollow thump of boots heading their way. Candy didn't hang around. Maddox would be back at his post anytime soon. And she had to be there to meet him. The door was dragged open.

'Where is the skunk now?' Steiner demanded in a guttural rasp.

'Right here,' Finn replied, kicking the door fully open and leaping into the room.

On seeing Finn, the bodyguard was momentarily stunned. But he soon recovered and launched himself at the intruder. But Finn was ready for the attack. He stepped to one side. The barrel of his revolver cracked against the thug's exposed head. Steiner crumpled in a heap.

Jardine was sitting behind his desk. For a brief moment he was speechless. Then he lurched to his feet.

'You again,' he rapped, a clawed hand reaching for a gun.

'Don't try it!' The terse command, brittle and laced with murderous intent stayed the grasping paw. Finn smiled. But there was no levity in the surly leer. 'You don't seem pleased to see me again, Jardine. Now I wonder why that can be?'

'What in thunder needs doing to get you out of my hair?' the gambler snarled, slowly sinking back into his seat.

'Just tell the truth. Your scheming rackets in Kansas City are over. I've had a wire from Ellsworth to say that Matt Sullivan is fully recovered and is ready to tell all he knows in a court of law.'

Jardine's mouth dropped open. He was rapidly arriving at the conclusion that the gravy train was heading for the buffers.

Finn then went on to stoke up the boiler.

'And not only that,' he continued leaning forward to reveal gritted teeth. 'Before he died under the wheel of the eastbound, Spike Dobey admitted that Harper was pulling all the strings.'

Finn paused to allow the full impact of his revelations to sink in. It was all a gigantic bluff. But Jardine did not know that.

Blood drained from the gambler's face. Sweat dribbled down his face. Finn's fervent need to frighten the gambler into admitting his part in the underhand practices blighting the city appeared to be working.

Lew Jardine was a big wheel in the lawless skulduggery. But he took his orders from Mister Big. He was the skunk Finn Dexter really wanted to bring down.

All the signs pointed to Silas Harper. However, without firm evidence the guy would remain free as a bird.

Steiner groaned as he slowly regained consciousness.

His head throbbed as he rubbed the swelling lump on his bullet head. But he remained tight-lipped. The German bodyguard was only a small fish in the organization and had no wish to dig himself into a deeper hole. All he could do for the moment was watch and wait, hoping to extricate himself from the mess at some point.

But with this heavyweight Pinkerton breathing down their necks, that possibility looked decidedly remote.

'The sheriff will be here any minute,' Finn snapped, waving his gun to dissuade them from any rash moves. 'You have one chance for a reduced sentence in the pen. And that's to reveal everything.'

The crux of his plan rested on forcing Harper's hand by drawing him out into the open. And Candy Stockwell was a key player in effecting that operation.

The singer was on tenterhooks after returning to the back door of the casino. She forced herself to assume a casual pose by leaning offhandedly against the wall. Yet inside, her heart was pounding like a Comanche war drum. It was a monumental struggle to maintain an outwardly serene appearance that would not arouse the suspicions of Bull Maddox when he returned.

The thump of boots heralded the guard's imminent arrival. She swallowed nervously while painting a bewitching smile on to her face.

Maddox was scowling. The search had taken him longer than he had wanted. But Candy was ready to counter any grumbling.

'The boss came by while you were away,' she

111

announced breezily. Maddox blanched. But the girl quickly allayed his qualms.

'Don't worry,' she gushed. 'I told him that I was standing in while you took a leak. He wants you to take this letter over to Senator Harper straightaway.' She handed over the letter given to her by Finn. 'And take a cab. Tell the driver to charge it to the casino.'

Maddox looked a mite bewildered at the sudden switch in his normal duties. Before he could voice any objections, Candy hustled him over to the back door.

'Straightaway,' she urged with a gentle nudge in the back. 'That was the order. So you need to get going pronto. You sure don't want to keep Mister Big waiting, do you, Bull?'

That was enough for Maddox. The last thing he wanted was to earn the boss's displeasure and end up like Rosco McGee when the boys had finished with him.

Once the coast was clear Candy closed the rear door but made sure it was left unlocked. Picking up her voluminous skirts, she hurried round to Jardine's office. There she listened at the door. It was clear that Finn had the gambler and his lackey covered, so she pushed open the door and went in.

'Everything worked just as you expected,' she assured Finn. 'Maddox has gone to deliver the letter.'

Jardine was splayed out in the seat behind his desk.

'So you're in on this too?' His sneering tone was chock-full of malicious accusation. 'I might have known a dame like you would betray me.'

'It's all over, Jardine,' Finn butted in. 'Best thing you can do now is confess the lot. When the sheriff arrives you'll have some tough questions to answer.' At that moment horses could be heard outside. 'That sounds like him now.'

Candy went back and ushered four men into the room. One of them was Ned Sullivan, who had decided that he wanted to be in the snake's den when the balloon went up. He was accompanied by the sheriff and his deputy. The fourth man was a grizzled oldster with the colourful handle of Big Nose Mike Whittle. He was the editor of the *Kansas Tribune*.

'Glad you are here, gents.' Finn thanked the visitors. 'You've arrived just at the right moment. Mr Jardine here has something to say that ought to prove mighty interesting.' Everyone focused on the morose gambling boss. Jardine slumped back, head in hands.

'All right, all right,' he burbled. 'I'll talk. But you have to speak up for me in court and tell the judge how I've cooperated fully.'

'That depends what you have to say,' growled Wild Bill Moody, the sheriff.

'Jumping Jericho! This is gonna be the story of the year,' enthused Big Nose Mike. A beaming grin split his wizened features.

His snout was no larger than a ripe plum, but the newspaper man had acquired the oddball moniker through his ability to sniff out all the best stories. Whittle licked the point of his pencil while readying himself for jotting down all the lurid details concerning the Kansas City rackets.

'OK then, Jardine, let's have all the juicy details,' he urged excitedly.

ELEVEN

THE TRAP IS SPRUNG

Senator Harper was shooting pool with one of his associates when Bull Maddox was ushered into the august presence. The burly ruffian had removed his hat and was shuffling his feet by the door, suitably overawed by the opulent surroundings in which he now found himself. There were few other residences in Kansas City that matched the ostentatious grandeur of Harper Heights.

Mouth agape, the bodyguard stared around.

This was another world to a guy brought up on the wrong side of the tracks. Snake Eyes was grand enough, but not a patch on this. The politician was living off the fat of the land and no mistake. And Maddox was well aware how this kind of lavish lifestyle had been funded.

Like the other bodyguards at Snake Eyes, he had

been grateful for a hitch up the social ladder that such a job gave him. A flashy suit and good grub, plus all the booze he could sink was worth safeguarding. All he had to do was look tough, strutting around the gambling rooms ensuring that everything ran smoothly.

Then that Pinkerton guy had come sniffing round. Suddenly everything was threatened.

Along with all the other guards, Maddox had strict instructions to shoot the guy on sight. The killing could easily be passed off as an accident. So far Dexter had not showed up. Perhaps he had been scared off. The jasper was like the cat with nine lives. He had the habit of keep turning up like a bad itch.

Anybody who could turn the tables on Panther Jack had to be taken seriously. Perhaps this letter would contain instructions of how the guy was to be eradicated.

Harper sniffed disdainfully. He recognized this odious specimen as being one of Jardine's stooges. So what was the guy doing sending messengers at this time of day?

'Have you something to say?' he demanded of the newcomer.

'A letter from the boss,' gurgled Maddox, gingerly stepping forward, hand outstretched. 'He said it was important.'

Harper frowned. He was a small, dapper man with a waxed moustache. His silk vest was stretched tight across an ample midriff, the result of easy living. Thin grey hair straggled down from a bald pate, giving him the appearance of a monk. But Silas Harper was no pious Bible-basher.

The envelope was blank. Quickly he extracted the missive and scanned the contents. With each line that he read his face grew redder. By the end steam was almost spouting from his dilated nostrils.

'This ain't from Jardine, you turnip,' he shouted, making Maddox jump. 'You've been played for a sucker. It's from that Pinkerton accusing me of being behind all the rackets in the city. He's claiming it was me that hired the gunmen, cos Matt Sullivan had discovered that me and Jardine were in cahoots.'

He threw the letter down and stamped round the room.

'What we gonna do, Senator?' asked one of his hired hands.

'Shut up and let me think,' snapped the politician. Then he stopped and addressed his next terse remark to Maddox. 'Has this guy been spotted around Snake Eyes?'

'Not for some time,' answered the bodyguard. 'All the doors are guarded and we have orders to shoot on sight if'n he does turn up.'

'What about Jardine? Where is he now?'

'Last I saw he was in the office checking the books with Steiner.'

Harper realized that he needed to get down to the casino pronto to make sure all their stories were watertight, that no loose ends were pointing his way. Once that tin star began snooping around, he could unearth all sorts of dirty laundry.

Damage limitation! That was the name of the game

now. This Dexter character was becoming a thorn in their sides. Standing around waiting for the varmint to show his hand was no good. He would have to be winkled out and dealt with permanently.

Jardine should have seen to that already. But he was letting the grass grow under his feet. Once again it was down to Silas Harper to take countermeasures. The senator grabbed his coat.

'Get my carriage ready,' he snapped out to his man. 'I'm going down to the Snake Eyes to see how much damage that fool has caused with his blundering.'

Ten minutes later the clarence was dashing madly through the streets of Kansas City, bound for the casino on the far side of town. Bull Maddox was up top, clinging on for dear life. Beside him, the whip cracked as the driver urged the team of four onward. The heavy carriage swayed and jolted its way along the rutted thoroughfares.

No thought as to the safety of other citizens was considered. Vociferous protests from pedestrians who were almost run down went unheeded. Even the pained squeal of a cat disappearing beneath the pounding hoofs failed to slow the vehicle's relentless onward speed.

Harper's sole intent was to reach the Snake Eyes before any harm was done to his reputation and illicit livelihood. The buffeting carriage finally skidded to an ungainly halt outside the rear door of the casino.

Harper jumped down and hurried inside.

In his office Lew Jardine was well into describing how Senator Harper was the ringleader of the underworld gang that was terrorizing the city. The threat of a long prison sentence was encouraging him to squeal like a stuck pig. He claimed to be just a small fish obeying the orders handed out by the crooked politician.

None of the watching sentinels had any doubt that this was true. Jardine was a devious scheming rat. But he was no Mister Big.

It turned out that Matt Sullivan had been at the Golden Garter saloon on Independence Street when he had become embroiled in a nasty piece of skulduggery. The young man was sussing out his next game on the craps table when he had accidently overheard a conversation that was meant to be distinctly private.

Inquisitive by nature, he sidled closer to a booth where the velvet drapes were drawn shut. Unseen, the occupants of the booth could still be heard. And there he stopped to listen in. What he learned was mind-blowing to a young man just out on the town hoping to enjoy himself.

A heist was being planned to snatch a payroll shipment. The details of the robbery were about to be divulged when Matt's eavesdropping was spotted. So intense was the eavesdropper's concentration that he had failed to notice one of Jardine's men keeping watch. Max Steiner quickly figured out what he was up to.

A shouted warning alerted the snooper, who realized his foolish error too late. Matt panicked and pulled a gun. The shot from his Colt Frontier missed Steiner, smashing a lantern instead. The return shot was better placed. The meddler was hit in the arm. More shots were exchanged.

Smoke filled the room. Panic ensued as the saloon's patrons dived for cover. Hidden among the mêlée, Matt was able to make his escape.

But he had been recognized. What the outlaw gang did not realize was that Matt had only heard snippets of the whispered conversation, and had no idea as to when or where the robbery was to take place. But they were taking no chances.

He would have to be eliminated.

Sheltering in his father's house offered only a temporary refuge. Soon or later, he would have to reveal himself, as the gang well knew. And the bandits would be ready. That was when Councillor Sullivan decided to spirit his son out of town. He arranged for the boy to stay with an old army friend on a cattle ranch near Ellsworth some 250 miles to the west of Kansas City.

Unbeknown to Ned Sullivan, they were followed to the railroad depot where a hired gunman also boarded the train to Ellsworth. That man was Cash Nagle.

Finn Dexter was listening intently to Harper's confession. It was Finn's subterfuge in spreading the word that Matt had cashed in his chips that had made the gang careless.

'Telling you all this is going to earn me a reduced sentence I hope, Sheriff,' Jardine pleaded.

Wild Bill was making no promises. He ignored the whining plea, gesturing for the gambler to continue with his confession.

Big Nose Mike was assiduously jotting down every word. His eyes bulged greedily, the trademark conk twitching like a Mexican jumping bean. Every revelation regarding the underhand enterprises in to which Senator Harper had dipped his greasy fingers was greeted with an uproarious chuckle.

'I reckon this is gonna go national,' Whittle declared. The ageing hack was becoming ever more animated.

That was the moment when Silas Harper burst into the room. At first he did not see the sheriff standing to one side. His whole being was focused on Lew Jardine, seated behind his desk in the middle of the room.

'You damn fool, Jardine,' he railed, waving the letter in his hand. 'What have you been saying? First you mess up that shooting of Matt Sullivan. Then you let slip all about our rackets in the city. This guy Dexter knows everything. We're gonna have to work out how we can fix him for good. . . .'

That was when he appeared to notice that the other people in the room were not members of the outlaw gang. His jaw dropped as his gaze lighted upon the sheriff's star. And beside him was the editor of the town's newspaper.

'Wha-what is all this?' he stammered.

'It's the story of the century, Senator,' shouted Whittle, leaping up and down. 'That's what it is. And all thanks to you and Jardine here. Jumping Jiminy! I'm gonna be famous.' The newspaper man's eyes misted over.

'And you're under arrest, Senator Harper,' announced Wild Bill Moody stepping out of the shadows. 'Clap the cuffs on him, Butte,' he ordered his deputy.

120

All eyes swung towards the burbling politician. Flecks of spittle ran down his double chin as he desperately attempted to extricate himself from the trap into which he had blundered.

Eventually finding his voice, the crooked official attempted to deny all knowledge of the accusations being hurled at him.

'This ain't what you think, boys,' he blethered. 'I'm here to help you guys.' But it was too late. The cat was out of the bag. Through his own mouth he had revealed the full extent of his chicanery. Witnesses were ready and willing to back up the charges in a court of law. The cuffs were slapped on to his wrists, hard eyes scornfully rejecting his weak-kneed disclaimers.

That was the moment when Jardine saw his chance of turning the tables. He lurched to his feet and grabbed Candy Stockwell. One hand roughly encircled her swanlike neck while the other palmed the revolver still lying on the desk. The gun barrel was jammed into the girl's cheek.

'Aaaaggggh!!' she screamed. 'Help . . .' The rest of the plea was choked off by a savage twist from Jardine's steely grip.

The terrified howl immediately captured the attention of the others.

Finn was the first to react on realizing what had occurred. He took a step forward.

'Harm one hair of her head and I'll kill you,' he snarled at Jardine.

The gambler's response was to let out a malicious guffaw.

'Not now that I'm holding all the aces, Pinky,' he growled. Then his tone hardened. 'Now drop that gun or the girl gets it.'

Finn hesitated. All his natural instincts screamed out that he should rush the critter. Flinty eyes arrowed hate at the leering gambler. It was Wild Bill who stayed the potentially fatal riposte.

'He means it, boy. The rat ain't got nothing to lose,' the ageing lawman cautioned in a calming monotone. 'So best do like he says.'

'The sheriff is a smart cookie.' Jardine's jabbing gun urged Finn to comply. 'Do what the wise man says if'n you want this cheating broad to see a new day.'

Finn scowled as Jardine tightened his grip on Candy's neck. But he reluctantly allowed the Peacemaker to slip from his grasp. The gambler's small yet deadly four-shot Lightning .41 then panned to cover the others.

'And the rest of you as well.'

Soon the room was once again under the control of the casino owner. Taking the cue from his boss, Max Steiner had drawn his own revolver to back him up.

'Collect up the hardware, Max,' Jardine snarled. 'We don't want these turkeys getting any bright ideas. Then empty the safe.' He delved into his pocket and produced a key. 'Guess the time has come for us to head for new pastures. Kansas City is becoming too darned hot.'

'What about me, Lew?' whined Harper. 'You can't leave me here like this after all we've been through.'

Jardine shrugged. 'Sorry about this, Senator.' His

apology was mocking and shallow. 'But you'll have to take your chances with all the rest . . .' His icy gaze then shifted to Bull Maddox who was expecting to ride out with Steiner and the boss. 'Just like this clown. It's on account of your bungling that we're in this mess now. All the dame had to do was flash her eyes and you fell for it. She tricked you so she could let these varmints in. There's only one answer to that.'

The double action revolver spat twice. Bull Maddox clutched at his chest as twin plumes of crimson spread rapidly across his white shirtfront. He staggered back, unable to comprehend what had happened.

'Is that dough sacked up?' Jardine snapped out to his associate.

'Sure is, boss.'

'Then let's ride.' The two outlaws backed towards the door. 'And remember, try to follow and Miss Stockwell here is the one that suffers.' The threat was aimed specifically at Finn Dexter.

Finn was frantic. Once the door had closed he made to cross the room. But again, it was Sheriff Moody who stopped him.

'You heard the skunk. I'm sure he will release Candy pretty soon. Carrying her along will only hold him up.'

But the assurance rang hollow. As long as the fugitives had the girl in their clutches, the forces of law and order were powerless to intervene. Yet still Finn voiced his apprehension.

'But he'll get away,' protested the frustrated Pinkerton, seething with anger.

TWELVE

THE WORM TURNS

'No he won't!'

This terse denial came from an unexpected source. The pursed lips of Senator Harper quivered. Here was his chance for revenge against that Judas of a partner. All eyes were now focused on the disgraced politician.

'You got some'n to say?' rasped Moody.

'Only if you promise to speak up for me in court.' Harper's beady eyes held those of the lawman. 'I know how Jardine's mind works. More than that, I know what he intends doing once he quits town.' His voice was steady, the consummate politician was once again making his play for support. 'So what do you say, Sheriff? Is it a deal?'

Moody was giving nothing away. His grizzled features remained unreadable.

'I ain't promising nothing,' he said. 'It all depends on what you have to offer. If'n you are able to assist the law in bringing these rats to justice, I'll make it my business to inform the court of any help you have given. But the judge will decide how to deal with you.'

That was all Harper could have expected. He nodded his acceptance.

'Jardine has a hideout in Stranger's Draw. It's two days' ride north-west of here.'

'Never heard of it.' Moody's reply was little more than a cynical grunt.

'That's because you'll know it by the name of Oskaloosa Creek,' replied the unfazed Harper. 'Ask anybody on the south side of town and they'll tell you it got the name because nobody goes up that way save hunters, army deserters and outlaws.'

'I can see how you would know that, Senator.' Moody's interruption was laced with irony, although he had adopted a more conciliatory tone.

Harper ignored the jibe as he continued: 'My reckoning is that he will hold the girl there as a hostage while he pulls the main job.'

'And what will that be?' enquired Moody, who had now taken more than a passing interest in what the crooked jasper had to say.

'He plans to rob the monthly payroll for the troopers at Fort Leavenworth.' This unexpected piece of news certainly received the undivided attention of the gathering. Harper's face broke into a pleased smirk.

'The dough is being taken up-river on the next paddle-wheeler leaving the dock terminal here in

Kansas City. And that's the *River Queen* in three days' time.'

This startling revelation received a series of startled gasps.

'You sure about this?' rapped the sheriff. Disbelief was written across the lawman's craggy face. 'Try pulling a fast one and I'll have you grafting on a chain gang for the next ten years.'

'Never more so,' came back the equally blunt retort. 'He plans to grab the dough when it leaves the steamer at Leavenworth dock. That was the plan Matt Sullivan is reckoned to have overheard in the Golden Garter.'

'If that's the case,' interrupted Finn, 'We ain't got a moment to lose. Can I make a suggestion, Sheriff?' Moody nodded for the younger man to continue. 'I have to agree with Harper. Jardine will keep hold of Miss Stockwell in case things go wrong with the robbery.'

He paused for Wild Bill's opinion.

'That's my view as well,' the sheriff concurred. 'What do you have in mind?'

'Leave straightaway and I could be at the draw when they set off to carry out the robbery. It's likely that only a token guard will be left with the girl. He can soon be taken care of. Then once the girl is safe I'll ride like the wind to Leavenworth dock and help you nail the critters. With you and a posse on board the steamer, I can add my weight from behind on the dock.'

Finn waited for Moody to consider the proposal. The sheriff was not slow in reaching a decision. A smile of agreement cracked his leathery façade.

'I can see why the Pinkerton Agency have signed you up, Finn. That sure is one humdinger of a plan.' He turned to address Butte Fender, his deputy. 'Go sign up a posse for a four-day trek. We need to be on the trail by noon.'

'What about me, Sheriff?' Harper whined. 'You won't forget my contribution, will you?'

A brittle order to his deputy followed as Wild Bill Moody headed for the door.

'Lock this turkey up and tell the jailer to watch him like a hawk while we're away. And make sure he enjoys a gourmet diet of bread and water.'

'You can't do that,' protested the aggrieved senator. 'I have my rights.'

Wild Bill nailed him with one of his most biting rejoinders.

'You threw them in the river by joining up with Jardine. Cheating the good folks of Kansas City comes at a heavy price, as you'll discover at your trial. You only blabbed to save your own miserable hide.'

His jabbing thumb indicated for his deputy to remove the disgraced toad. 'Now get this piece of garbage out of my sight.'

Fender's stubbled face broke into an impish grin. 'Be my pleasure, Sheriff.' His firm hand grabbed the politician by the scruff of the neck. Fender then brusquely hustle him outside.

It was Finn who called for Fender to hold on.

'How do I reach Stranger's Draw?' he asked the sheriff.

Moody replied with a negative shrug, then added, 'But that skunk will know.'

Harper was dragged back into the office.

'Right, mister, how do I get there?' Finn snapped out.

Under no illusions that he was heading for a spell in the Kansas pen, Silas Harper was reluctant to reveal the location of the hidden draw. He wanted solid promises of clemency. A discreet glance of understanding passed between Finn and Sheriff Moody, who now left the casino office along with his deputy. Their next task was to question the rest of the staff.

Flexing the bulging muscles beneath his grey flannel shirt, Finn advanced on the quaking crook.

'Now are you going to give me directions to find Stranger's Draw, or do I have to beat it out of you.'

Delivered in a low, even tone, the threat sounded all the more menacing. It was matched by a hard glint from flinty eyes that held no hint of mercy.

Harper was left in no doubt that this guy meant business. The crook made a feeble show of resistance.

'You can't manhandle a state senator,' he burbled. 'The law forbids it.'

But his spirit soon crumbled when Finn grabbed hold of his suit and shook him like a dog with a bone. Buttons popped as the senator's ruffled shirt was torn open.

'I'm judge and jury in here,' rasped Finn. 'So talk, or my law will be administered.'

The jasper was no hero. His strength came out of the mouth, not the end of a gun. The necessary information

128

was soon bubbling forth in a torrent.

'All right,' Finn called out. 'You can come back in now.'

Back in the office, Moody threw a scornful glare at the morose politician.

'OK, Butte, take him away.' Then he hitched up his gunbelt. 'Let's hope that this time we can finally rid the town of its plague of vermin. And if'n we're successful it'll be you that I'll have to thank.'

He held out a hand. The two men shook. Each was praying that Finn's plan would be pulled off. Yet neither was under any false illusions that blood would be spilled before the final reckoning could be assured. All they could hope for was that it would be shed by the outlaws.

The line of riders were trailing the west bank of Oskaloosa Creek. Lew Jardine was in the lead. Behind him was a horse carrying the captive singer. Bringing up the rear were another seven men recruited by Max Steiner when he had detoured into the town of Lawrence. Jardine had made camp in a dry wash outside the town to prevent his hostage raising the alarm.

Throughout the trek Candy made surreptitious efforts to delay their journey to the outlaw hideout of Stranger's Draw by gently pulling back on the sorrel's reins. But the gang boss had become aware of her stratagem.

'Keep that up and I'll have Max here tie you face down over the saddle,' came the furious threat. 'I'm sure he'd enjoy that.'

A lascivious grin split the bodyguard's ugly visage. Candy shivered. She knew there was no further chance of delaying the inevitable any longer.

Towards the middle of the second day they hauled rein outside a cave in the cliff face overlooking the shallow watercourse. Inside it was dry with a couple of side passages that had been converted into bunk rooms. All the cooking was done on a fire at the far end of the main cave where an open flue to the bluffs above allowed the smoke to escape. The water supply was obtained from Oskaloosa Creek. The accommodation was basic which, being temporary, was all that was required of it.

Candy was immediately put to work cleaning up the cave. It had clearly not been used for some months. The previous occupants had left it in a mess. That would not normally have bothered a bunch of hard-nosed brigands, but Jardine and his buddy had become used to an easier way of living at Snake Eyes. Their noses wrinkled at the foul reek of rotten food and stale liquor that hung in the fetid air.

The men were also hungry after their hard ride. Providing for seven hard-nosed brigands made yet another onerous task for Candy. Luckily, the boss had arranged beforehand to stock the place with plenty of tinned grub and tobacco. But no hard liquor. The men had to be sober for the coming job.

Over the next two days Candy's delicate hands became red raw from the household chores and constant preparation of meals. It didn't help that she was regarded as a menial skivvy at the beck and call of these uncouth braggarts. Jardine was no better than the others. Gone were the civilized manners and decorum adopted while running Snake Eyes. He had reverted to his lowlife roots.

But at least he made sure the men kept their physical desires in check. Any untoward bawdy moves were instantly quashed. The bossman knew that his hostage had to be kept presentable in case his plans for the robbery went awry.

During the period spent in the cave before the fateful day of the robbery, Jardine ensured that his men were kept busy. By the time they left Stranger's Draw on the morning of the third day, each man knew exactly what was expected of him. Guns had been cleaned and oiled, the proposed course of action assiduously practised.

A rustler by the name of China John was left behind to keep an eye on their hostage. The villain had acquired his name after a bout of yellow jaundice had left his face permanently discoloured.

Jardine made abundantly clear what would happen should he return to find Candy Stockwell in any condition other than how he had left her.

What the gang did not realize when they mounted up and left the cabin was that their progress was under close scrutiny.

Finn had made good time. He was crouched behind some rocks on a bluff overlooking the cave below. Regrettably, from his position it was impossible to see inside the dark opening. A direct approach up Oskaloosa Creek would have been out of the question. He would easily have been spotted. A detour along the upper edge of the valley was the only way of getting close enough to the cave.

Finn was forced to wait there until the gang left before making his rescue bid. Yet even as they pulled out, he still had not figured out how best to neutralize the guard.

Once the gang had disappeared down the draw he peered over the rim of the bluff. A narrow path threaded its way down to ground level. But following that would leave him exposed, out in the open, a sitting target.

There had to be an easier way of winkling the rat out of its hole. An hour later and he still had not come up with a workable plan. Time was passing. He was becoming frustrated. Walking along the edge of the cliff, he desperately cudgelled his brain.

Then he noticed a thin plume of smoke drifting up from a dark hollow some fifty feet back from the edge. It looked like a hole in the rock. As he hurried across it soon became evident that the fissure was indeed a vertical shaft. It was blackened around the edges. Scraping it with his finger revealed soot that could only have come from a fire. Feeling less cautiously around the edge Finn found that it was cool.

This must be a chimney flue for the occupants of the cave. Luckily it was not being used. But that state of affairs could change at any moment. He peered into the grimy opening. It was dark and dirty, but there appeared to be plenty of hand- and footholds.

A way out of his situation had presented itself. But it would be a hazardous undertaking that had little appeal. However, with no other apparent means of achieving his goal, and time fast running out, this was his only chance of freeing Candy Stockwell.

Girding himself for the grim task, Finn began the tricky descent. Extreme care was needed so as not to dislodge any loose stones that would alert the guard below. In no time Finn was covered in a cloying film of soot. His mouth and nose became filled with the noxious grunge. Keeping his eyes tight shut was no impediment in the pitch blackness of the flue.

Slowly he descended into what felt like the bowels of hell.

Each step had to be gingerly tested, hand holds firmly placed. After what seemed like a full lunar cycle, he tentatively opened one eye and peered upwards. The small circle of blue informed him that he must be over halfway down. Not much further to go. Voices drifted up through the dense black fog. One was gruff. It was followed by the instantly recognizable cadence of Candy Stockwell.

At least he now knew his supposition regarding Jardine's intentions was correct.

A dim glow appeared below. He was almost at the makeshift fireplace. He lowered one hand to feel the comforting presence of the Colt Peacemaker on his hip. A few more steps and he was ready to make his play.

He braced himself, breathed deep, then dropped the five remaining feet into the ashes of the dead fire.

The crash of splintering burnt wood fragments, along with a rattling displacement of stones, echoed round the bare rock walls of the cave.

'What in tarnation is that?' a tremulous voice blurted out. To both occupants of the cave it sounded like the roof was collapsing in on them.

'It's Old Nick come to collect his dues,' growled the terrifying spectacle that had emerged from the dark opening at the rear.

The guard was stunned into frozen immobility.

His mouth gaped wide at the sight of this terrifying apparition. The likeness to the devil in the fertile imagination of China John was horridly convincing. The spectre, hunched, with red eyes glaring and white teeth gleaming from a soot-blackened face, advanced into the open.

It was the revolver clutched in the devil's hand that shunted John's bemused brain back into the real world. His face twisted, knowing he had been hoodwinked by his own innate fears. This was no demonic spectre from the underworld, but an intruder come to rescue his hostage.

That deduction was confirmed when the spectre once again spoke up.

'Drop your gun, mister. Or pay the devil's price.' The smiling ogre advanced a step further. The double click of the six-shooter's hammer brought the guard finally back to the real world.

China John stiffened. He was undecided. Should he surrender, or take the chance of drawing on this dude? It had worked before, when the Texas Kid had had the drop on him. That had been last year in Wichita. A quick dive to one side, pistol palmed and it had been goodbye Texas.

In the few moments during which China John was considering his options, he had forgotten about the presence of Candy Stockwell. She could sense that he was wondering whether to go for his gun. Now she saw a means of helping her benefactor before that decision was made.

Gently edging over behind the guard, she reached out and snatched the pistol from its holster before China John had a chance to draw. He let fly a startled yelp, knowing he had been tricked. Yet again. This time by a woman.

John's shoulders slumped. He sank down into a chair, thoroughly deflated. All the stuffing had been knocked out of him.

In a matter of minutes Finn had him securely pinioned.

Candy could not contain her elation at being rescued, and by none other than Finn Dexter.

'I had given up all hope when Jardine brought me here,' she said, rushing into the arms of her guardian angel. They clung together, disregarding the presence of the morose outlaw. 'How did you find me? He said this place was known only to him and the gang.'

'Harper spilled the beans, hoping to get off with a lenient term in jail,' Finn replied stroking the trembling girl's silken tresses. 'But you're safe now.' Then he drew away. Much as he craved to linger in the company of this divine female, duty still called.

'We need to hit the trail pronto. Jardine is planning to lift an army payroll from the *River Queen*. It's due in Leavenworth Dock tomorrow around noon. I promised Sheriff Moody I'd be there to help him prevent the heist.'

Following the long ride to Stranger's Draw, and his nerce-racking descent of the flue, Finn was exhausted. Candy recognized that he needed a rest and some grub. She had been about to make a stew for herself and China John when Finn had dropped in. The simple yet wholesome fare was soon prepared and consumed.

An hour later they were on the trail. The nearest town with a law office was Muskotah.

Their first call was at the jail, where China John was left in the capable hands of Marshal Tiny Lomas. A giant of a man, Lomas was as black as the ace of spades. He had come West after the war and soon established a reputation for meting out summary justice. To the ex-plantation slave, sporting the revered tin star of a lawman was a personal vindication of the Northern victory in the Civil War.

China John was given suitable lodgings in the one available cell. It so happened that the outlaw had a price of $300 on his head, which Finn arranged to collect on his way back from Leavenworth.

Candy was offered far more agreeable accommodation at the Occidental Hotel.

The two starry-eyed lovers were reluctant to separate. The next part of Finn's plan was the most hazardous.

Going up against a ruthless gang of robbers was no Sunday picnic. Worry was etched across the girl's weary

136

features as they said their farewells. But speed was of the essence; the girl would slow Finn down. He promised to come back for her as soon as the robbery had been thwarted.

THIRTEEN

EYE ON THE DOCKS

Lew Jardine arrived at Leavenworth Dock in plenty of time to organize his men. The *River Queen* was not due for another two hours. All the robbers were clad in the traditional garb of dock labourers, making them indistinguishable from the real workers. Their guns were concealed beneath coats as they hefted bales and shifted cargo about so as not to attract unwelcome attention.

The only fly in the ointment as far as Jardine was concerned was a lack of any accomplices on the paddle-wheeler. He had hoped to have two men aboard as back-up when the heist was made. But that interfering Pinkfoot had put paid to that. All their efforts would need to be focused on the landing party.

According to inside information from an accounts clerk at Fort Leavenworth, four blue-coats were escorting the money.

An ululating series of mournful hoots heralded the arrival of the *Queen*. The shallow-draft vessel had twin red smokestacks and independent side-wheels. One of many such craft that plied up and down the Missouri River, she carried all manner of cargo as well as passengers. Heaps of wood were piled high on the lower deck to feed the insatiable boilers. Even then, the *Queen* had to stop each day to take on extra supplies.

This was her first outing with a new boiler, the old one having exploded on the previous trip killing five crew members and three passengers. Despite the dangers, the paddle steamers remained a popular method of travel, being both speedy and comfortable.

Once a landing was imminent Wild Bill Moody positioned his four-man posse at the front of the ship. They were hidden behind bollards and cotton bales. The four troopers mounted up, surrounding the mule that carried the two strongboxes containing the money.

The ship gently nosed up to the wooden jetty, where dock workers secured the thick hawsers. Once the passengers had disembarked it was the turn of the four troopers. Guns at the ready, the hidden posse followed their progress as one by one the horsemen stepped on to the jetty.

So far everything was going according to plan.

Screwing up his eyes, Wild Bill scanned the dock area for any suspicious movement. Yet, try as he might, he was unable to perceive anything untoward. If the information Harper had supplied was genuine, this was where the heist would take place. So where were Jardine and his bunch hiding? The sheriff was growing more restive by the second. The veins in his neck twitched. Not a good sign.

The payroll escort was now on the jetty attempting to control a wayward mule that had become skittish when it slipped on the narrow gangplank. It was now thrashing around in the shallows. Two of the troopers were struggling to calm the frantic beast while the others hunkered down on the jetty, keeping watch.

That was when the gang made their move.

At a signal from Jardine, who was hidden behind some barrels, his men threw off their thick reefer jackets. Guns appeared in their hands as they opened fire on the exposed troopers. The noise was deafening. Any passengers still in the vicinity scattered. Only the real dockers remained, now easily distinguished from their bogus counterparts. Panic spread like wildfire as they dropped flat on to the wooden decking. Heads down, they then began crawling into any available cover.

One of the soldiers had gone down in the initial volley, hit by three bullets. Tumbling off the jetty, the riddled body was soon swallowed up by the Missouri mud. Another grabbed his rifle and began firing blindly into the gun smoke. But unlike the gang, he was out in the open, a sitting duck. He didn't stand a chance. Only the pair hidden by the jetty were able to carry on the fight.

In the meantime, Wild Bill and his men had opened up from the deck of the *River Queen*.

'Watch for their smoke, boys,' he yelled out. 'Then make every shot count.' He snapped off a quick shot at one jigger who had raised his head too high above a cotton bale.

'Yahooooo!' came the elated holler from the sheriff as the outlaw threw up his arms. 'See what I mean, boys?' His voice rose excitedly above the din.

The battle raged on, the crackle of gunfire filling the air. Lead was flying everywhere. Sharp reports from small arms were interspersed with the deep-throated roar from rifles. There were even blasts from shotguns. One such removed the head of another outlaw foolish enough to show himself.

But those on the river boat were effectively pinned down by the volleys from the remaining outlaw guns. Jardine was an effective organizer and had his men spread out in strategic positions. Moody's posse did, however, have the advantage of unlimited ammunition. One thing Jardine lacked.

He had been caught out by the ferocious response from the vessel, for which he had not bargained. Somehow they must have found out about the robbery. This was turning into a much more hazardous enterprise than he had calculated for. Continue exchanging fire like this and they would soon run short of ammunition.

Then he cursed his foolishness, comprehension dawning as to what had occurred.

Harper! The treacherous skunk must have ratted on them, hoping to save his own skin. The gang leader cursed again, knowing he should have killed the senator while he had the chance. Too darned late for regrets now.

Then a scream rattled his eardrums. Max Steiner had gone down only a couple of feet from where Jardine was standing. This was getting too hot. It was time to pull out. There would always be other hold-ups once he regrouped. Wasn't it better to run away to fight again another day than brave it out for nothing more than a plot on boot hill?

But all that lovely dough was still down there within his reach. Leaving it behind was entirely at odds with the brigand's nature. Greed stayed his hand. The problem was how to grab the loot with all this lead flying around. There had to be a way.

A brainwave struck him with the force of a kicking mule. The analogy extracted a tight smirk as the perfect solution presented itself. It was the recalcitrant mule that put the idea into his head.

The animal had moved away from its military keepers, whose attention was solely concentrated on staying alive. Just to encourage them in that endeavour, Jardine emptied his spare revolver at the cringing blue-bellies.

The mule took the opportunity to further distance itself from the fracas. Slowly the beast moved closer towards the spot where Jardine was hidden.

'Come on, my beauty,' he excitedly cajoled the stub-born critter. 'Another few yards and you're mine.'

He aimed a couple more bullets just to the rear of the mule, encouraging it to shift further in his direc-tion. The outlaw couldn't resist a howl of glee. It was time to move.

Loyalty to his remaining men was tossed in the river.

142

It was now a question of winner takes all and every man for himself. Lew Jardine meant to secure that prize and had no intention of sharing it out. Having made the decision, he now put it into operation.

One man amidst the carnage of Leavenworth Dock would have no problem slipping away unseen. Gingerly he crawled out from where he was concealed and hurried down to the waterfront, where he hid in a clump of dwarf willow. As the mule passed he took hold of its rein and gentle guided the animal into the shelter of the trees. The two strongboxes were still securely strapped to its back.

A couple of well-placed bullets smashed the locks. The noise was lost amidst the continuing cacophony. Inside the boxes were stacked piles of greenbacks. Jardine's greedy peepers briefly scanned the money before it was transferred to his saddle-bags. The horse being close by, he was able to slip away undetected. At first it was necessary to lead the animal on foot to avoid being spotted from the paddle-wheeler.

Once he was through the riverside willows a dense tangle of thorn bushes and shrubs tore at his clothing. Thereafter he was thankfully able to disappear over the embankment built up to counter the frequent flooding of surrounding land. He lost no time in mounting up and spurring off back to Stranger's Draw.

Only a fluke prevented Finn Dexter from encountering the fleeing outlaw on the trail. His horse had thrown a shoe some five miles west of Leavenworth, close to the town of Tonganoxie. He left the animal with the blacksmith who promised to have a new shoe fitted within the hour. Meanwhile, Finn retired to a nearby diner for some much needed rest and refreshment.

It was bad luck that his horse had thrown the shoe. The delay was frustrating. Hunched over his meal, Finn's thoughts centred on the girl and what she now meant to him.

That was the moment when Lew Jardine trotted down Tonganoxie's single street. Had Finn looked idly out the window, he might have seen his adversary passing by, although it is highly unlikely that he would have recognized him. Jardine's usual natty appearance had been substantially altered since his fleeing Snake Eyes. The battle at Levenworth Dock had left him dishevelled and down at heel, no better than a saddle tramp. But the avaricious glint in his eyes was unmistakable.

So it was that ten minutes later Finn collected his mount and continued along the road to Leavenworth. Jardine, meanwhile, was heading in the opposite direction.

By the time Finn reached the dock, the last of the surviving outlaws had been mopped up. With their leader mysteriously absent, control of the fight had disappeared. Those left were like headless chickens, unable to think for themselves. Their urge to continue the fight rapidly disintegrated as chaos reigned.

Wild Bill rallied his men and rushed the few remaining gang members, who threw up their arms and surrendered. But of their leader there was no sign. More important, there was no sign of the payroll. It soon dawned on the lawman that his quarry had landed a hard sucker punch.

An utterly mortified Bill Moody was forced to concede that he had been tricked. When Finn arrived the sheriff was sitting on a cotton bale. Shame and humiliation registered on the old lawdog's haggard features as he glumly explained how he had managed to lose the payroll. It was hard for a man of Wild Bill's reputation to acknowledge that he had been thwarted by a lowlife braggart of Jardine's ilk.

Not one readily to cast blame, Finn knew exactly what needed to be done.

'Don't worry, Sheriff,' he consoled the distraught lawman. 'You've split up the gang and Candy Stockwell is safe. I left her in a hotel over in Muskotah, along with the guard who is occupying less agreeable lodgings at the town jail.' He quickly explained the circumstances of the one-man raid on Stranger's Draw.

Learning of Finn's success only served to remind the lawman of his own ineptitude. But Finn's priority now was to stop the gang leader from escaping with the payroll.

'How much of a start do you figure he has?'

Wild Bill forced himself to shrug off the lethargy that was threatening to swamp him. He was a professional and needed to act like one. His men still looked to him for leadership.

'Far as I can judge he must have quit the dock about two hours ago.'

'Jardine will have headed back to Stranger's Draw hoping to pick up the girl,' Finn hurried on. 'He thinks she is still being held there as a hostage. Toting all that dough will slow him up. On a fresh mount I could beat him to it.'

'Bring that money back, Finn,' urged a re-energized Bill Moody, 'and I'll make sure you get the full reward that has been put up.'

Finn's primary interest, however, was in enhancing his career prospects with Allan Pinkerton. Monetary considerations came second. There was also the exciting prospect of having Candy Stockwell at his side in this new life.

FOURTEEN

NO SWEET FOR CANDY

Muskotah had grown to prominence at a vital crossing point where the Vermillion and Oskaloosa Creeks merged. This, however, was of no importance to Lew Jardine. His primary interest was in the town's bank, which was the only building constructed of brick. It offered a robust stability that gave confidence to those opting to make use of its facilities.

As such it was just what the outlaw was seeking. Not to rob. For once the bank was to be exploited for legitimate purposes.

The money stuffed to the brim in his saddle-bags needed to be off-loaded. Carrying that amount of dough around was inviting trouble, especially from members of his own kind. The notion of loyalty among thieves was a myth, pure make-believe, as he had so amply demonstrated by ditching his men on Leavenworth Dock. Not only that, the excessive weight was slowing him down.

He halted briefly, therefore, to stock up on travelling goods and maybe allow himself a couple of drinks to celebrate his good fortune. For Lady Luck had indeed been watching over Lew Jardine.

He swung over to a vacant hitching rail outside the Occadillo Hotel, dismounted and tied off. That was when he received a startling jolt to his feel-good mood.

There, next to his own horse, was another that he instantly recognized. Stepping round, he examined the markings carefully. The sorrel mare had white feet and a distinctive grey mark on her rump. No doubt about it. This was the mount ridden by Candy Stockwell. So how in the name of Jacob had this nag got here?

China John should be holding the girl on a tight rein in the cave. Had she worked her female wiles on the knucklehead and escaped? Or had the skunk decided to try his own luck at hostage negotiation? This latter seemed far too outlandish for a moon-calf like China John. There had to be some other explanation. And Lew Jardine intended to seek it out pronto.

The person likely to know every newcomer in town was the local bartender. Those guys were founts of information, which they were always prepared to share at a price. Jardine dipped into one of the bags and extracted a wad of notes – his working capital. Then he sauntered across the street to the Plainsman saloon. The place was full of dirt farmers. The surrounding grasslands were being ploughed up for maize. Jardine ambled up to the bar and ordered a beer.

'And one for yourself, barman,' he said, slapping a ten spot down on the counter. Straightaway, he had created the right impression. Fatback Slim smilingly pulled the drinks and accepted the banknote. Then came the announcement that all barmen dream about but few encounter. An invitation to '. . . keep the change.'

Another tenner then slid across the counter.

'Maybe you could tell me if there have been any strangers in town over the last couple of days?' Jardine's hand rested firmly on the note as he waited for the reply. 'And if'n it's the right answer,' Jardine murmured in a conspiratorial whisper, 'there'll be another of these coming your way.'

Fatback's eyes popped. That was two weeks' pay for an assistant barman. Beads of sweat bubbled on his upper lip. He idly brushed them away. What was this guy's angle? But he thought better of asking. Even though shabby and unkempt, the stranger was no common drifter, not with dough like that to spare.

'A fella passed through here two days ago. He had brought an owlhoot in and left him with the town marshal. There was also a fancy-looking dame with him.'

Jardine stiffened. 'What was this guy like?'

The barman considered. 'A tall, rangy dude dressed all in black. He was a tough-looking jasper who carried himself like he knew where he was headed. Once he'd settled the girl in the hotel across the street, he called here for one drink then left.'

So, Jardine mused, that nosy Pinkerton had sussed out his hideout and even gone so far as to rescue the girl. The skunk was a boil that needed lancing. Another thought then flashed through his brain. Maybe they had even passed each other on the trail. At least it looked as if the girl was still in town. That was a stroke of good fortune. What to do about it, though? That was the question he now faced.

Jardine lifted his hand, allowing the banknote to quickly disappear.

'Are you a jasper that can be trusted to keep his mouth shut?' he rasped, fixing a beady eye on the barman, a look that promised dire consequences should that trust be betrayed.

'You bet, mister,' was the eager response. 'Anything you want, Fatback Slim is your man.'

Yet another ten bucks changed hands as Jardine outlined exactly what he wanted the barman to do. He finished his drink, then left and went straight across to the bank to make his deposit. The reason given for such a large amount of loose cash was that his father had died and left him the family farm, which he had sold.

Within two hours of entering Muskotah he was riding out the far side. But only as far as a cluster of cottonwoods that surrounded an open glade some three miles to the west. Here he settled down to kill time before putting his plan into effect.

He didn't have long to hang around. Hoofbeats penetrated the tree cover. Jardine smiled, stepping back into the verdant gloom. Fatback Slim appeared to have wasted no time in carrying out his instructions.

Moments later, a familiar horse entered the glade. As expected, it was Candy Stockwell in the saddle. She was clad in riding gear, comprising split leather skirt, flannel shirt and fringed vest, all topped off with a wide-brimmed tan Stetson. No doubt about it, she was a tasty dame, a cut above the usual broads he employed. She would look good on his arm in Santa Fe.

The girl trotted to the centre of the open sward and peered around. Uncertainty was painted across the smooth features. Where was Finn? She had received the message while lunching in the hotel restaurant. Shrugging aside the outlandish nature of the request to meet him at the cottonwood grove as soon as possible, she had left the dessert of apple pie and cream untouched. So why was he not here to meet her?

That was when another figure stepped into the open. Lew Jardine held his gun steady as a rock.

'Guess you weren't expecting to see me again, eh Candy?' His tone was bright and breezy, as if they were old friends who hadn't met up in a while. 'Dexter was unavoidably detained. I'm taking his place.'

Candy was dumbfounded. She was given no time to figure out what had happened.

'You and me are going for a little ride. A big one actually,' he continued, mounting up. The pistol remained firmly in place. 'We are heading south-west to a little place I've bought down in Santa Fe. Whether you reach my new hacienda in one piece depends on how well you behave.' The gun wagged menacingly. 'And if'n we meet any . . . erm, problems along the way. . . .'

He was referring to the pursuit that might follow. Although confident that nobody was aware of his destination, he knew that Wanted posters would soon be pinned to the walls of every law office from Missouri to the Rio Grande. But Jardine had always believed in not playing his hand without some form of back-up. Candy Stockwell would be that counterweight.

'You'll never get away,' she blurted out.

'I already have,' Jardine laughed. It emerged as a throaty cough. 'And with all that lovely dough from the payroll robbery, which is now sitting in a bank earning interest. You can be a part of my success, be an important *señorita* if'n you cooperate, Candy. But play me false and I might be forced to terminate our association ... permanently.' The threat was punched out, brittle and unambiguous.

'What happened to Finn?' Candy swallowed nervously. She was loath to hear the answer to her query. Jardine's reaction was something of a relief.

'Ain't seen hide nor hair of that skunk since I butted out from Snake Eyes. Like as not he'll be running around the territory now like a scalded cat. Playing the Good Samaritan by rescuing you wasn't such a good deal after all, was it? 'A hoot of laughter followed this viewpoint. He didn't wait for a reply.

'OK, let's go.'

He gestured for her to lead the way.

Two hours later Finn Dexter rode into Muskotah. He headed straight for the Occidental Hotel. Discovering the subterfuge that had been played was a shock to the system. By some freak of chance, Jardine had discovered Candy's presence in the town and lured her into a trap.

There was no denying that the guy was a shrewd operator, more cunning than a wily coyote. He had sadly underestimated the critter's determination to slip the net. It had been a bad mistake to assume the gang boss would head direct for Stranger's Draw to lie low for a few weeks until the hue and cry had died down.

He could be anywhere now. With Candy as a hostage he had a bargaining chip, should the net of pursuit tighten around him.

Finn was disconsolate. How was he going to find a needle in a haystack?

Then a thought occurred to him. Wasting no further time in self-recrimination, he pushed on down the street to the town marshal's office.

FIFTEEN

SHOWDOWN AT BOGDEN'S HOLE

The answer could lie with China John, who was locked up in the town hoosegow.

Marshal Tiny Lomas was ready with his reward money. Finn thanked him but stuffed it in his pocket unchecked. He had other more important issues in mind.

The incarcerated owlhoot saw no point in holding out on the tough Pinkerton. He revealed that Jardine had bought a hacienda near Santa Fe. His plan was to head down there once the heist had been pulled off.

So elated was Finn by this revelation that he left China John with some dollar bills with which to purchase a more stimulating diet than the usual prison slop. Knowing that Jardine was only a couple of hours ahead, he pushed on without delay.

He headed direct for the cottonwoods where Candy had gone for her fateful meeting. It was easy to pick up the trail from there.

An important part of Pinkerton training had been in the art of tracking and picking up sign. An old Comanche chief called Grey Owl had been hired to pass on all his skills to the new recruits. Finn Dexter was an avid learner. He now proceeded to put the newly acquired skill to good use.

Three sets of tracks led out of the grove, joining the main trail west towards Topeka. If what China John had divulged was correct about a protracted journey into New Mexico, then the third animal must be a pack animal. The small party had followed the main trail west for only a short distance before branching off to follow a less-used but parallel route.

Jardine clearly did not want to encounter other travellers whom his prisoner might be tempted to alert to her plight. But, being a much less travelled highway, this side trail offered easier sign to track. It was evident that only two riders and a smaller animal had passed this way in the recent past. Broken twigs, trampled grass, horse dung and water splashes on rocks told their own story; all vital indications that Finn was closing on his quarry.

Finn would have thoroughly enjoyed putting his newly acquired proficiency into practice had he not been so concerned for Candy's safety. Nevertheless, he still relished the chase. Each new discovery elicited a self-indulgent hoot of glee. Even the grim circumstances of his quest failed to stifle a professional enjoyment in spotting the vital clues that would eventually frustrate the pesky varmint's plans. Lew Jardine was going to have the shock of his life when Finn Dexter spiked his guns.

The sun was dipping towards the western horizon when he crested a low rise. Down below in a hollow could be seen the spiralling plume of a newly lit fire. He drew to a halt. Jardine must have decided to make camp for the night. Finn dismounted, extracted a pair of binoculars from his pack and scanned the locality, searching for any movement. He was soon able to focus on one of the riders who was unpacking the bedrolls and cooking gear from a packmule.

Jardine was unrecognizable as the casino dandy with which Finn was familiar. But there was no mistaking the elegant sway of Candy Stockwell as she sashayed down to the nearby creek to carry out her ablutions. He longingly followed her sinuous movements before she disappeared into the undergrowth.

Finn placed his hands together and gave silent thanks to a higher power for guiding him to this lonely place.

Now he would have to work out how he was going to undertake yet another rescue plan. He swept his binoculars slowly across the surrounding terrain. He did not know it, but this was the source of Soldier Creek, a major Kansas tributary of the mighty Missouri River.

Irregular clusters of rock enclosed the hollow, below which was a circlet of trees comprising hickory, oak and cottonwoods. And there at the heart of the hollow was a swamp of choked reeds and clinging mud.

Bogden's Hole was well named. Its smooth, deceptive surface was ever ready to swallow up any careless intruder that ventured within its odious grasp. Few who braved the treacherous invitation had ever escaped.

The campsite was adjacent to the hole on a flat stretch of sand. Candy had avoided the main bog, opting for the cleaner trickle of spring water flowing from surrounding rocks. Perhaps she sensed the aura of menace emanating from the threatening morass.

Finn decided to move in closer on foot.

Cautiously he slowly descended a faint deer track. However, it soon faded and he was forced to descend a steepening slope of shifting gravel. Care was needed to keep his footing as he negotiated a way through a thick press of thorny bushes that sought to impede his passage. A couple of buzzards circled overhead, curious voyeurs to this strange spectacle being played out in their domain.

The tricky descent ended abruptly by the dense reedbeds of the swamp. Finn shivered. He circled round the edge of the fetid bog losing sight of the camp momentarily. A foul odour of rotting vegetation lay heavy in the air.

With the Peacemaker gripped firmly in his right hand, the stalker crept in closer until he reached the edge of the clearing. There he paused. Over on the far side, the prone figure of Lew Jardine appeared to be asleep beside the fire.

With the outlaw's back to him, Finn saw this as a golden opportunity to surprise the varmint. He stepped out into the open and catfooted across the clearing.

Halfway over, a harsh cough from behind brought him to a sudden halt. As he was about to turn around a well-known voice froze him in his tracks.

'Stay right where you are, Pinky, and don't move a

blamed muscle.' The brusque crackle of the order had caught him out. 'You are becoming a huge embarrassment to my reputation.'

Finn cursed his ineptitude. He had been duped.

A hoarse cackle echoed all around. 'Guess you're wondering how I got the drop on you?'

'Guess I am at that.' Finn's upbeat reply was a forced attempt to hide his chagrin at being bested.

'Take a closer look at those duds,' Jardine scoffed. 'and you'll see that my hat is propped up on the saddle with a few branches covered by a blanket. Looks mighty convincing from a distance, don't you think?' He didn't wait for a reply. 'The old tricks are the best, eh? I learned it from Jesse James himself.'

Finn issued a curse under his breath. 'And I expect you're wondering how I managed to find you?' He was playing for time, hoping that some miracle would enable him to wriggle out of the tight spot into which he had blundered.

'My big mouth again,' the outlaw reproved himself with a grunt of disdain. 'That Judas China John must have squealed.'

Then he continued with his explanation.

'You were a mite noisy coming down that back slope,' Jardine chided. He was thoroughly relishing the crafty ruse he had pulled. 'Sound carries far in Bogden's Hole. So I knew you were coming.' The hammer of the crook's revolver snapped to full cock. 'The time for jawing is over, Mister Smarty Pants. Nobody gets the better of Lew Jardine and lives to tell the tale.'

Finn held his breath. Any second and it would be all

over. Another frustrated oath hissed from between clamped teeth. Then it came. A sharp blast ripped apart the silence of the Hole. The lights went out.

Night had laid its enveloping mantle over Bogden's Hole when Finn Dexter slowly surfaced. His eyes flickered open. Was he in Heaven or Hell? It sure didn't feel like he was labouring for the Devil. A soothing balm was being gently massaged across his head.

He tried to lift himself but a lilting murmur eased him back down. In the soft flicker from the firelight, a vision of beauty blocked out the myriad twinkling stars. The radiant features of Candy Stockwell then swam into view.

'Where am I?' he croaked.

'Keep still,' came the mellifluous yet imperious tone. 'You've lost a lot of blood. But you were lucky that the bullet only creased your scalp.'

'What about Jardine?' Finn garbled, his eyes staring in shocked disbelief.

But the effort was too much. He lapsed back into unconsciousness.

Only in the light of the new day was he able to fully learn what had happened. A bandage was wrapped around his head, which throbbed abominably. It felt like a mule was hammering to get out. But he was alive, and so was Candy. After a cup of strong coffee and some vittles, he was ready to hear the bizarre circumstances of how he had come back from the dead.

Candy had heard the commotion and emerged from the creek behind where the two men were standing. Knowing that Jardine was about to shoot, she had grabbed a loose branch and sneaked up behind him.

The blow had stunned the outlaw, but not before he managed to pull the trigger.

Candy had struck him again then pushed him over. Jardine had staggered back to escape her assault and slipped on some wet leaves close to the edge of the swamp. He had lost his balance and tumbled into the morass. Barely a minute later his thrashing body had completely disappeared beneath the clutching reeds. Only a few bubbles signified his passing from this mortal coil.

Bogden's Hole had claimed another victim.

'It was horrible,' the girl sobbed. 'Nobody should have to end their days like that.'

Finn took her in his arms. 'It's all over now, Candy. We're both safe.' He swallowed, delaying what he wanted to say. A tense silence followed.

'Have you something else you want to say?' Candy enquired, a wry smile creasing her delicate features.

'Well . . .' he hesitated, his rugged features assuming the colour of an ocatillo flower. 'I was wondering if when we get back to civilization, you might . . . well . . . consider walking out with me. Maybe we could . . .'

She placed a finger over the trembling lips. 'I'd be more than honoured.'

Finn sighed.

Suddenly, Bogden's Hole wasn't so vile after all. Indeed it seemed like the most desirable place in the world. A sweet-smelling nirvana. Finn Dexter closed his eyes, a smile of contentment easing away the hammer inside his head.